"Unnamed blade, I call thee Corum's sword!"

Corum heard Goffanon's song, in the far distance:

> *"Here is a fitting sword,*
>   *Half mortal, half immortal,*
> *For the Vadhagh hero.*
>   *Here is Corum's sword.*

> *"There is no comfort in the blade I made,*
>   *It was forged for more than war;*
> *It will kill more than flesh;*
>   *It will grant both more and less than death…"*

When the song ended, Corum raised the sword high over his head and said in a quiet, firm voice: "I am Corum. This is my sword. I am alone…"

MICHAEL MOORCOCK

THE SWORD AND THE STALLION

BERKLEY BOOKS, NEW YORK

FOR JUDITH

THE SWORD AND THE STALLION

A Berkley Book / published by arrangement with
the author

PRINTING HISTORY
Berkley Medallion edition / April 1974
Berkley edition / December 1986

ISBN: 0-425-09391-3

THE SWORD AND THE STALLION

THE CHRONICLE OF PRINCE CORUM
AND THE SILVER HAND

Being a History in Three Volumes of what befell the Vadhagh Prince, Corum Jhaelen Irsei (who is also called the Prince in the Scarlet Robe), after the Tale of the Sword Rulers, already recorded as the Books of Corum.

Volume the Third

THE SWORD AND THE STALLION

by Michael Moorcock

PROLOGUE

In those days there were oceans of light and cities in the skies and wild flying beasts of bronze. There were herds of crimson cattle that roared and were taller than castles. There were shrill, viridian things that haunted bleak rivers. It was a time of gods, manifesting themselves upon our world in all her aspects; a time of giants who walked on water; of mindless sprites and misshapen creatures who could be summoned by an ill-considered thought but driven away only on pain of some fearful sacrifice; of magics, phantasms, unstable nature, impossible events, insane paradoxes, dreams come true, dreams gone awry, of nightmares assuming reality.

It was a rich time and a dark time. The time of the Sword Rulers. The time when the Vadhagh and the Nhadragh, age-old enemies, were dying. The time when Man, the slave of fear, was emerging, unaware that much of the terror he experienced was the result of nothing else but the fact that he, himself, had come into existence. It was one of many ironies connected with Man (who, in those days, called his race Mabden).

The Mabden lived brief lives and bred prodigiously. Within a few centuries they rose to dominate the westerly continent on which they had evolved. Superstition stopped them from sending many of their ships toward Vadhagh and Nhadragh lands for another century or two, but gradually they gained courage when no resistance was offered. They began to feel envious of the older races; they began to feel malicious.

The Vadhagh and the Nhadragh were not aware of this. They had dwelt a million or more years upon the planet, which now, at last, seemed at rest. They knew of the Mabden, but considered them not greatly different from other beasts. Though continuing to indulge their traditional hatreds of one another, the Vadhagh and the

Nhadragh spent their long hours in considering abstractions, in the creation of works of art and the like. Rational, sophisticated, at one with themselves, these older races were unable to believe in the changes that had come. Thus, as it almost always is, they ignored the signs.

There was no exchange of knowledge between the two ancient enemies, even though they had fought their last battle many centuries before.

The Vadhagh lived in family groups occupying isolated castles scattered across a continent called by them Bro-an-Vadhagh. There was scarcely any communication between these families, for the Vadhagh had long since lost the impulse to travel. The Nhadragh lived in their cities built on the islands in the seas to the northwest of Bro-an-Vadhagh. They, also, had little contact even with thier closest kin. Both races reckoned themselves invulnerable. Both were wrong.

Upstart Man was beginning to breed and spread like a pestilence across the world. This pestilence struck down the old races wherever it touched them. And it was not only death that Man brought, but terror, too. Wilfully, he made of the older world nothing but ruins and bones. Unwittingly, he brought psychic and supernatural disruption of a magnitude which even the Great Old Gods failed to comprehend.

And the Great Old Gods began to know fear.

And Man, slave of fear, arrogant in his ignorance, continued his stumbling progress. He was blind to the huge disruptions aroused by his apparently petty ambitions. As well, Man was deficient in sensitivity, had no awareness of the multitude of dimensions that filled the universe, each plane intersecting with several others. Not so the Vadhagh or the Nhadragh, who had known what it was to move at will between the dimensions they termed the Five Planes. They had glimpsed and understood the nature of many planes, other than the five, through which the Earth moved.

Therefore it seemed a dreadful injustice that these wise races should perish at the hands of creatures who were still little more than animals. It was as if vultures feasted on and squabbled over the paralyzed body of the youthful poet who could only stare at them with puzzled eyes as they slowly robbed him of an exquisite existence they would never appreciate, never know they were taking.

"If they valued what they stole, if they knew what they were destroying," says the old Vadhagh in the story, 'The Only Autumn Flower', "then I would be consoled."

It was unjust.

By creating Man, the universe had betrayed the old races.

But it was a perpetual and familiar injustice. The sentient may perceive and love the universe, but the universe cannot perceive and love the sentient. The universe sees no distinction between the multitude of creatures and elements which comprise it. All are equal. None is favored. The universe, equipped with nothing but the materials and the power of creation, continues to create: something of this, something of that. It cannot control what it creates, and it cannot, it seems, be controlled by its creations (though a few might deceive themselves otherwise). Those who curse the workings of the universe curse that which is deaf. Those who strike out at those workings fight that which is inviolate. Those who shake their fists shake their fists at blind stars.

But this does not mean that there are some who will not try to do battle with and destroy the invulnerable.

There will always be such beings, sometimes beings of great wisdom, who cannot bear to believe in an insouciant universe.

Prince Corum Jhaelen Irsei was one of these. Perhaps the last of the Vadhagh race, he was sometimes known as the Prince in the Scarlet Robe.

This is the second chronicle concerning his adventures. The first chronicle, known as The Books of Corum, told how the Mabden followers of Earl Glandyth-a-Krae killed Prince Corum's relatives and his nearest kin and thus taught the Prince in the Scarlet Robe how to hate, how to kill, and how to desire vengeance. We have heard how Earl Glandyth tortured Prince Corum and took *away a hand and an eye and how Corum was rescued by the Giant of Laahr and taken to the castle of the Margravine Rhalina—a castle set upon a mount surrounded by the sea. Though Rhalina was a Mabden woman (of the gentler folk of Lywm-an-Esh), Corum and she fell in love. When Glandyth roused the Pony Tribes, the forest barbarians, to attack the Margravine's castle, she and Corum sought supernatural aid and thus fell into the hands of the sorcerer School, whose domain was the island called Svi-an-Fanla-Brool—Home of the Gorged God. And now Corum had direct experience of the morbid, unfamiliar powers at work in the world. Shool spoke of dreams and realities ("I see you are beginning to argue in Mabden terms," he told Corum. "It is just as well for you, if you wish to survive in this Mabden dream." "It is a dream . . . ?" said Corum. "Of sorts. Real enough. It is what you might call the dream of a god. There again you might say that it is a dream that a god has allowed to become reality. I refer of course to the Knight of the Swords, who rules the Five Planes.")*

With Rhalina his prisoner, School could make a bargain with Corum. He gave him two gifts—the Hand of Kwll and the Eye of Rhynn—to replace his own missing organs. These jeweled and alien things were once the property of two brother gods known as the Lost Gods, since they had mysteriously vanished.

Armed with these, Corum began his great quest, which was to take him against all three Sword Rulers—the Knight, the Queen, and the King of the Swords—the mighty Lords of Chaos. And Corum discovered much concerning these gods, the nature of reality, and the nature of his own identity. He learned that he was the Champion Eternal, that, in a thousand other guises, in a thousand other ages, it was his lot to struggle against those forces which attacked reason, logic and justice, no matter what form they took. And, at long last, he was able to overwhelm (with the held of a mysterious ally) those forces and banish gods from his world.

Peace came to Bro-an-Vadhagh and Corum took his mortal bride to his ancient castle which stood on a cliff

10

overlooking a bay. And meanwhile the few surviving Vadhagh and Nhadragh turned again to their own devices, and the golden land of Lwym-an-Esh flourished and became the center of the Mabden world—famous for its scholars, its bards, its artists, its builders, and its warriors. A great age dawned for the Mabden folk; they flourished. And Corum was pleased that his wife's folk flourished. On the few occasions when Mabden travelers passed near Castle Erorn he would feast them well and be filled with gladness when he heard of the beauties of Halwyg-nan-Vake, capital city of Lwym-an-Esh, whose walls bloomed with flowers all year round. And the travelers would tell Corum and Rhalina of the new ships which brought great prosperity to the land, so that none in Lwym-an-Esh knew hunger. They would tell of the new laws which gave all a voice in the affairs of that country. And Corum listened and was proud of Rhalina's race.

To one such traveler he offered an opinion: "When the last of the Vadhagh and the Nhadragh have disappeared from this world," he said, "the Mabden will emerge as a greater race than ever were we."

"But we shall never have your powers of sorcery," answered the traveler, and he caused Corum to laugh heartily.

"We had no sorcery at all! We had no conception of it. Our 'sorcery' was merely our observation and manipulation of certain natural laws, as well as our perception of other planes of the multiverse, which we have now all but lost. It is the Mabden who imagine such things as sorcery—who would always rather invent the miraculous than investigate the ordinary (and find the miraculous therein). Such imaginations will make your race the most exceptional this Earth has yet known, but those imaginations could also destroy you!"

"Did we invent the Sword Rulers whom you so heroically fought?"

"Aye," answered Corum, "I suspect that you did! And I suspect that you might invent others again."

"Invent phantoms? Fabulous beasts? Powerful gods?

11

Whole cosmologies?" said the astonished traveler. *"Are all these things, then, unreal?"*

"They're real enough," Corum replied. *"Reality, after all, is the easiest thing in the world to create. It is partly a question of need, partly a question of time, partly a question of circumstance . . ."*

Corum had felt sorry for confounding his guest and he laughed again and passed on to other topics.

And so the years went by and Rhalina began to show signs of age while Corum, near-immortal, showed none. Yet still they loved each other—perhaps with greater intensity as they realized that the day drew near when death would part her from him.

Their life was sweet; their love was strong. They needed little but each other's company.

And then she died.

And Corum mourned for her. He mourned without the sadness which mortals have (which is, in part, sadness for themselves and fear of their own death).

Some seventy years had passed since the Sword Rulers fell and the travelers grew fewer and fewer as Corum of the Vadhagh people became more of a legend in Lwyman-Esh than he was remembered as a creature of ordinary flesh. He had been amused when he had heard that in some country parts of that land there were now shrines to him and crude images of him to which folk prayed as they had prayed to their gods. It had not taken them long to find new gods and it was ironic that they should make one of the person who had helped rid them of their old ones. They magnified his feats and, in so doing, simplified him as an individual. They attributed magical powers to him; they told stories of him which they had once told of their previous gods. Why was the truth never enough for the Mabden? Why must they forever embellish and obscure it? What a paradoxical people they were!

Corum recalled his parting with his friend, Jhary-a-Conel, self-styled Companion to Champions, and the last words he had spoken to him: *"New gods can always be* created," he had said. Yet he had never guessed, then, from what at least one of those gods would be created.

And, because he had become divine to so many, the people of Lywm-an-Esh took to avoiding the headland on which stood ancient Castle Erorn, for they knew that gods had no time to listen to the silly talk of mortals.

Thus Corum grew lonelier still; he became reluctant to travel in Mabden lands, for this attitude of the folk made him uncomfortable.

In Lwym-an-Esh those who had known him well, known that, save for his longer lifespan he was as vulnerable as themselves, were now all dead, too. So there were none to deny the legends.

And, likewise, because he had grown used to Mabden ways and Mabden people about him, he found that he could not find much pleasure in the company of his own race, for they retained their remoteness, their inability to understand their situation, and would continue to do so until the Vadhagh race perished for good. Corum envied them their lack of concern, for, though he took no part in the affairs of the world, he still felt involved enough to speculate about the possible destiny of the various races.

A kind of chess, which the Vadhagh played, took up much of his time (he played against himself, using the pieces like arguments, testing one strain of logic against another). Brooding upon his various past conflicts, he doubted, sometimes, if they had ever taken place at all. He wondered if the portals to the Five Planes were closed forever now, even to the Vadhagh and the Nhadragh, who had once moved in and out of them so freely. If this were so, did it mean that, effectively, those other planes no longer existed? And thus his dangers, his fears, his discoveries, slowly took on the quality of little more than abstractions; they became factors in an argument concerning the nature of time and identity and, after a while, the argument itself ceased to interest Corum.

Some eighty years were to pass since the fall of the Sword Rulers before Corum's interest was to be reawak-

ened in matters concerning the Mabden folk and their
gods.

And this interest was awakened in a strange way when
Corum heard voices in his dreams. The voices craved his
help and called him a god, called him Corum Llaw Ereint—Corum of the Silver Hand. And Corum denied the
voices until Jhary-a-Conel, his mysterious old friend who
seemed able to cross between the planes at will, advised
him to heed their call, for they were the descendants of
Rhalina's own folk—the folk of Lwym-an-Esh. For
Corum was the Champion Eternal and it was his fate to
fight in all the great wars involving the most crucial and
profound events in mankind's destiny.

So at last Corum agreed and he garbed himself in all
the martial finery of the Vadhagh and he strapped on
the best of his artificial silver hands (which could perform all the functions of a fleshly hand) and he went
riding on a red horse into the future to meet the folk of
Cremm Croich and to battle the horrible Fhoi Myore,
the Gods of Limbo, the Cold Folk, the People of the
Pines.

He found a world attacked by winter—a world fast
freezing to death as the Fhoi Myore drew all heat from
the land, wherever they conquered; and they poisoned
whatever they conquered, without thought for their own
existence, for they were moved by primal desires, not by
intelligence, and they desired death. Many of the Mabden folk had already perished and the treasures of the
Mabden had been stolen or scattered and their Great
Kings had been slain or captured or sent into hiding.
And only a few small tribes in the remote West or in the
distant North had not yet been in conflict with the Fhoi
Myore—seven gods in seven crude wicker chariots drawn
by seven foul beasts, seven gods who could destroy whole
armies with a glance and those leader was Kerenos, who
controlled a pack of hellish hounds.

From King Mannach of Caer Mahlod, from Medhbh,
the king's daughter, Corum learned that only the Black
Bull of Crinannass could drive off the Fhoi Myore in
some unknown way. And the woman was fair, this

Medhbh, and she was strong and a warrior and Corum was reminded of Rhalina, his dead love, and he was stirred by Medhbh.

He was told of his quest. His quest was to the land of Hy-Breasail, beyond the sea. This land was enchanted and no mortal returned from it. But Corum, they said, was a god, a Sidhi. He could go to Hy-Breasail.

And so he went. Through a winter world he went (though it was not winter time) and had many adventures, encountered many strange folk, talked with wizards and with Sidhi, made bargains, and heard a prophecy. An old woman warned him that he should fear *a harp, a brother, and beauty.* Corum was puzzled by the prophecy and particularly puzzled as to why he should fear beauty. But he went on to Hy-Breasail, the only remaining part of sea-covered Lwym-an-Esh, and there he found the spear, Bryionak, one of the lost treasures of the Mabden which could, in the right hands, control the Black Bull. And many more adventures followed until he returned to Caer Mahlod as the Fhoi Myore attacked in all their dreadful might—seven malformed gods, together with their servants, the lost, the evil, the damned and the undying, led by Corum's old enemy Prince Gaynor, who could not be slain but yearned for death. And there was a battle at Caer Mahlod and the battle went ill for the Mabden until the Bull was summoned and drove off the Fhoi Myore's undead slaves and slew one of those crude, cruel gods and caused the others to flee.

Then the final rite took place and the land was made green again around Caer Mahlod and the Black Bull of Crinnanass and the spear, Bryionak, were never again seen in mortal lands.

And Corum and Medhbh lay together in love, but still Corum brooded on the prophecy for he knew he was the Champion Eternal and as doomed to struggle as was Prince Gaynor.

And the Fhoi Myore, the Lost Gods of Limbo, remained upon the Earth.

Thus it was at last that the Great Red King, King Fiachadh of the Tuha-na-Manannan, the people of the

Distant West, came a-visiting with his splendid retinue, to confer with King Mannach and debate the matter of the Fhoi Myore. Already King Fiachadh had visited the kings of the surviving Mabden lands—Tuha-na-Anu, the land south of his own; Tuha-na-Tir-nam-Beo in the north; Tuha-na-Gwyddneu Garanhir, the land nearest that of the Tuha-na-Cremm Croich. King Fiachadh urged his fellow kings to unite against the Fhoi Myore in one last attempt to drive them away forever, but his fellow kings were cautious, saying that with their High King, Amergin, a prisoner of the Fhoi Myore there was none to command them. The only thing which would unite the Mabden, said King Fiachadh, would be the release of Amergin and the restoration of his full senses.

So Corum said that he would try to rescue Amergin and this was to King Fiachadh's liking and King Fiachadh gave Corum a gift to help him enter Caer Llud where the Fhoi Myore now ruled and where Amergin was an enchanted prisoner. This gift was one of the old treasures of the Mabden, a tattered Sidhi cloak which made certain wearers invisible: Arioanrod's Cloak.

Corum set off upon the second of his Quests, swearing that he would return with Amergin or not return at all.

Corum had not been long upon his Quest when he met his old enemy Gaynor, who refused to fight him, and his old friend Jhary-a-Conel, the self-styled Companion to Heroes, who aided him against the Hounds of Kerenos. Together they continued for Caer Llud, through lands bearing much evidence of Fhoi Myore desecration. And it grew colder, and Gaynor and his hounds still tracked them, and once Corum heard the mysterious harp playing again and was afraid. Then they came to Craig Don.

Craig Don was the great holy place of the Mabden—seven circles of tall stones, each circle containing another until at the center there lay a large stone altar—and Corum fancied the stone circles represented ripples upon a pool, planes of reality, representations of a geometry not wholly connected with Earthly geometry. And Corum wondered if this place might not be the Mabden's Tanelorn, for though the place was primitive in its materials it was considerably subtle in its conception. This had been the center of the Mabden world.

And here, while they rested near the altar, came Gaynor, believing this place to be their ultimate destination and unwittingly revealing that the Fhoi Myore feared the properties of the place. "The vortex," he said, "cannot swallow Gaynor the Damned."

Then Gaynor revealed his trap. The Hounds of Kerenos circled Craig Don. Corum and Jhary could not leave. They would starve there unless Gaynor brought them food. They were his prisoners forever. But by skill and cunning they did escape, after Gaynor had gone, and continued their journey, arriving at last in Caer Llud and seeing much evidence that the Fhoi Myore prepared to make war on the Mabden again. This lent further urgency to their activities. After considerable difficulty and danger Amergin was rescued, though still enchanted and believing himself to be a sheep, and an old friend, Goffanon, was discovered to be an enemy when he attacked Corum with his axe. It then emerged, however, that Goffanon was under a spell, too—a slave of the Wizard Calatin, who had used Goffanon's spittle to ensnare the Sidhi dwarf, who had traded Corum the Sidhi horn in exchange for his name-robe, his Scarlet Robe, and who now leagued himself with the Fhoi Myore. Fleeing Caer Llud with Amergin, fleeing the wrath of Calatin and the Fhoi Myore, Corum was able to rescue—albeit temporarily—Goffanon from the spell. Then they all went back to Craig Don and here Jhary made an incantation, reaching for Amergin's mind through the many veils of the enchantment, learning what they must do to rid him of that enchantment. He could be released only through the power of the Oak and the Ram—only the Oak Woman could call him home.

Now they must go to Tuha-na-Gwyddneu Garanhir, where the Golden Oak and the Silver Ram were thought to reside. While Jhary-a-Conel took Amergin to Caer Mahlod, Corum and Goffanon would go by sea to Gwyddneu Garanhir.

17

They were at sea when it became evident that the Fhoi Myore traveled, too, to Gwyddneu Garanhir, bent on conquest. Further dangers were met before they reached a place where the People of the Pines waited for them. Attacked, all seemed lost, but then came help in the form of a golden god, a tall, laughing warrior who brought with him the smell of the sea, a giant, much taller than Goffanon—one of the surviving Sidhi, the son of the famous Manannan. Ilbrec he was named and he bore his father's sword Retaliator and he rode a huge horse called Shining Mane. And he had been unwittingly awakened by the Fhoi Myore and he was angry. So he helped them. And thus three Sidhi warriors arrived at Caer Garanhir with the dread news of the Fhoi Myore's coming.

It was ill-received, that news, and King Daffyn was drunk, as were all the warriors of Caer Garanhir, for they celebrated the marriage of the king's son. Yet somehow—for all it seemed Ilbrec deserted them in his disgust—they defended the city when the Fhoi Myore came. Many good knights died. There was much tragedy, King Daffyn's being the most intense. But at last, equipped with the twin Treasures of Llud, the Oak and the Ram, they made speed back to Caer Mahlod, having received King Daffyn's word that, if Amergin were revived, he would follow the High King against the Fhoi Myore.

But before they could return there were further strange adventures, one of which involved Calatin, who was able to re-exert his power over Goffanon, and another of which involved Sreng of the Seven Swords, one of the Fhoi Myore, who died at last with delight. And five Fhoi Myore were now left upon the earth.

Then the three—Corum of the Silver Hand, the Dwarf Goffanon, and the Sidhi youth Ilbrec—came to Caer Mahlod. And the time was growing short and it seemed that Amergin was almost dead.

So they took Amergin to a place of power, to Cremmsmound, when the moon was at its fullest and shone upon the oaks of the grove and upon the white mistletoe, and here Corum shivered and recalled Ieveen's prophecy concerning what he must fear.

At night, in the grove, the rituals and the summonings began, while what remained of Amergin's life ebbed away. Goffanon sang a song and found a word and when he spoke the word it made Corum gasp and an awful shock ran through his whole body and he staggered, his heart pounding and his head swimming, though the word meant nothing to his conscious mind. The word was "Dagdagh."

And when the word was spoken the harp began to play. It was the same harp Corum had heard more than once before and heard at its most fearsome in his dreams. And this was the sound of the Dagdagh harp, which most thought stilled forever. But only Corum feared the sound. All others were grateful to it, for it seemed to call the Oak Woman and the Oak Woman was able to revive Amergin and restore him to his whole sanity in the strangest of all the rituals Corum had so far witnessed.

And when she had revived Amergin the Oak Woman spoke to Corum: "You are Corum. You saved the High King and you found the Oak and the Ram. You are the Mabden Champion now. You shall be great in the memories of this folk, yet you shall know little lasting happiness here. Your destiny is a noble one."

And then the Golden Oak, the Silver Ram and the Oak Woman were gone and were never afterward seen again in mortal lands.

Yet Corum was haunted by the name of the Dagdagh harp which Goffanon said was an old name and a title, too, perhaps. Not a Sidhi name, though associated with the Sidhi. And Goffanon recalled a hint of a story regarding the Dagdagh's having betrayed the Sidhi cause during one of the historic nine fights against the Fhoi Myore.

Then, while all others celebrated, Corum left the hall of the king and went out to where he could stand looking over the gulf separating him from Castle Erorn, his

19

old home, which was now called Castle Owyn. And he thought he saw a face staring at him from one of the broken windows of the castle. A handsome face, a face with a skin of gold; a mocking face. And when Corum called "Dagdagh!" he was answered by laugher which became the music of the harp.

He drew his sword, calling: "Dagdagh, let me be!"

Then came Medhbh to his side, saying: "Dagdagh is our friend, Corum. Dagdagh saved our High King."

But Corum knew Dagdagh was not his friend.

And that was the end of the Tale of the Oak and the Ram. And now the news went to all the surviving Mabden that the High King was restored and that they must mass at Caer Mahlod, there to begin their last great war against the Fhoi Myore.

> THE CHRONICLE OF CORUM AND THE
> SILVER HAND

BOOK ONE

In which armies are gathered and
plans debated regarding an assault
upon the Fhoi Myore and Caer Llud.
Sidhi advice is requested and gladly
given; yet, as is often the case, the advice creates further perplexity.

The First Chapter

CONSIDERING THE NEED FOR GREAT DEEDS

So they came to Caer Mahlod; all of them. Tall warriors garbed in their finest gear, riding strong horses, bearing good weapons. They had a look of practical magnificence. They made the country around Caer Mahlod blaze with the bright colors of their samite pavilions and their embroidered battle flags, the gold of their bracelets, the silver of their cloak clasps, the burnished iron of their helmets, the mother-of-pearl inlaid upon their carved beakers or set into their traveling chests. These were the greatest of the Mabden and they were also the last, the People of the West, the Stepsons of the Sun, whose cousins of the East had long since perished in fruitless battle with the Fhoi Myore.

And in the center of their encampments stood a tent much larger than the rest. Of sea-blue silk, it was otherwise unadorned and no battle banner stood near its entrance, for the size of the tent alone was enough to announce that it contained Ilbrec, the son of Manannan-mac-Lyr, who had been the greatest of the Sidhi heroes in the old fights against the Fhoi Myore. Tethered near this tent stood a huge black horse, large enough to seat the giant; a horse of evident intelligence and energy: a Sidhi horse. Though welcome in Caer Mahlod itself, Ilbrec could find no hall high enough to contain him and had thus pitched his tent with those of the gathering warriors.

Beyond the fields of pavilions there were green forests of pleasant trees, there were gentle hills dotted with clumps of wild flowers and shrubs whose colors sparkled like jewels in the warming rays of the sun; and to the west of all this glowed a blue, white-crested ocean over which black and grey gulls drifted. Though they could not be seen from the walls of Caer Mahlod, there were many ships on all the nearby beaches. The ships had come from the isle of the west, bringing the folk of Manannan and Anu; they had come from Gwyddneu Garanhir and they had come from Tir-nam-Beo. They were ships of several different designs and divergent purposes, some being warships and others being trading ships, some used for fishing the sea and some for traveling broad rivers. Every available ship had been utilized to bring the Mabden tribes to this massing.

Corum stood upon Caer Mahlod's battlements, the Dwarf Goffanon at his side. Goffanon was a dwarf only by Sidhi standards, being considerably taller than Corum. Today he did not wear his polished iron helm; his huge unkempt mane of black hair flowed down his shoulders, meeting his heavy black beard so that it was impossible to tell which was which. He wore a simple smock of blue cloth, embroidered at collar and cuffs in red thread and gathered at the waist by his great leather belt. There were leggings and high-laced sandals on his legs and feet. In one huge, scarred hand was a mead horn from which he would sip occasionally; the other hand rested on the haft of his inevitable double-bladed war-axe, one of the last of the Weapons of Light, the Sidhi weapons especially forged in another Realm to fight the Fhoi Myore. The Sidhi dwarf looked with satisfaction upon the tents of the Mabden.

"They still come," he said. "Good warriors."

"But somewhat inexperienced in the kind of warfare we contemplate," Corum said. He watched as a column of northern Mabden crossed the ground beyond the main gate and the moat. These were tall and tough, in scarlet plaids which made them sweat, in winged or horned helmets or simple battle-caps; red-bearded men for the most part, soldiers of the Tir-nam-Beo, armed with big broadswords and round iron shields, disdaining all other weapons save the knives sheathed in the belts which criss-crossed their chests. Their dark features were painted or tattooed in order to emphasise their already fierce appearance. Of all the surviving Mabden, these men of the high northern mountains were the only ones who still lived, for the most part, by war, cut off by their own chosen terrain from what they regarded as the softer aspects of Mabden civilization. They reminded Corum somewhat of the old Mabden, the Mabden of the Earl of Krae who had hunted him once across these same downs and cliffs, and for a moment he wondered again at his willingness to serve the descendants of that cruel, animal-like folk. Then he recalled Rhalina and he knew why he did what he did.

Corum turned away to contemplate the roofs of the fortress-city of Caer Mahlod, leaning his back against the battlements, relaxing in the warmth of the sunshine. It had been over a month since he had stood at night upon the brink of the chasm separating Castle Owyn from the mainland and shouted his challenge to the Dagdagh harpist whom he was convinced inhabited the ruin. Medhbh had worked hard to console him and make him forget his nightmares and she had been largely successful; he now saw his experiences in terms of his exhaustion and his dangers. All he had needed was rest and with that rest had come a certain degree of tranquility.

Jhary-a-Conel appeared on the steps leading to the battlements. He had on his familiar slouch hat, and his little winged black and white cat sat comfortably on his left shoulder. He greeted his friends with his usual cheerful grin. "I've just come up from the bay. More ships have arrived—from Anu. The last, I heard. They have none left to send."

"More warriors?" said Corum.

"A few, but mainly they bring fur garments—all that the people of Anu can muster."

"Good." Goffanon nodded his great head. "At least we'll be reasonably well-equipped when we venture into the Frostlands of the Fhoi Myore."

Removing his hat, Jhary wiped sweat from his brow. "It's hard to imagine that the world is so cold such a comparatively short distance from here." He put his hat back on his head and reached inside his jerkin, taking out a piece of herbal wood and broodingly picking his teeth with it as he joined them. He stared out over the encampment. "So this is the whole Mabden strength. A few thousands."

"Against five," said Goffanon, almost defiantly.

"Five gods," said Jhary, giving him a hard stare. "In keeping our spirits high we must not let ourselves forget the power of our enemies. And then there is Gaynor— and the Ghoolegh—and the Pine Warriors—and the Hounds of Kerenos—and," Jhary paused, adding softly, almost regretfully, "and Calatin."

The dwarf smiled. "Aye," he said, "but we have learned how to deal with almost all these dangers. They are no longer quite the threat they were. The People of the Pines fear fire. And Gaynor fears Corum. And as for the Ghoolegh, well, we still have the Sidhi Horn. That gives us power, too, over the hounds. As for Calatin . . ."

"He is mortal," said Corum. "He can be slain. I intend to make it my particular business to slay him. He has power only over you, Goffanon. And, who knows? that power could well be on the wane."

"But the Fhoi Myore themselves fear nothing," said Jhary-a-Conel. "That we must remember."

"They fear one thing in this plane," Goffanon told the Companion to Heroes. "They fear Craig Don. It is what we must ever remember."

"It is what they ever remember, also. They will not go to Craig Don."

Goffanon the Smith drew his black brows together. "Perhaps they will," he said.

"It is not Craig Don, but Caer Llud we must consider," Corum told his friends. "For it is that place we shall attack. Once Caer Llud is taken, our morale will rise considerably. Such a deed will give our men increased strength and enable them to finish the Fhoi Myore once and for all."

"Truly great deeds are needed," Goffanon agreed, "and also cunning thoughts."

"And allies," said Jhary feelingly, "more allies like yourself, good Goffanon, and golden Ilbrec. More Sidhi friends."

"I fear that there are no more Sidhi save we two," murmured Goffanon.

"It is unlike you to express such gloom, friend Jhary!" Corum clapped his silver hand upon the shoulder of his companion. "What causes this mood? We are stronger than we have ever been before!"

Jhary shrugged. "Perhaps I do not understand the Mabden ways. There seems too much joy in all these newcomers, as if they do not understand their danger. It is as if they come to a friendly tourney with the Fhoi Myore, not a war to the death involving the fate of their whole world!"

"Should they grieve, then?" Goffanon said in astonishment.

"No . . ."

"Should they consider themselves in death or in defeat?"

"Of course not . . ."

"Should they entertain one another with dirges rather than with merry songs? Should their faces be down-turned and their eyes full of tears?"

Jhary began to smile. "You are right, I suppose, you monstrous dwarf. It is simply that I have seen so much. I have attended many battles. Yet never before have I seen men prepare for death with such apparent lack of concern."

"That is the Mabden way, I think," Corum told him. He glanced at Goffanon, who was grinning broadly. "Learned from the Sidhi."

"And who is to say that they prepare for their own deaths and not the deaths of the Fhoi Myore?" added Goffanon.

Jhary bowed. "I accept what you say. It heartens me. It is merely that it is strange and the strangeness is doubtless what I find discomforting."

Corum was, himself, disconcerted to find his normally insouciant friend in such a mood. He tried to smile.

"Come now, Jhary, this brooding demeanor suits you ill. Normally it is Corum who mopes and Jhary who grins . . ."

Jhary sighed.

"Aye," he said, almost bitterly, "it would not do, I suppose, to forget our roles at this particular time."

And he moved away from them, pacing along the battlements until he reached a spot where he paused, staring into the middle distance, plainly desiring no further conversation with his comrades.

Goffanon glanced at the sun.

"Nearly noon. I am promised to advise the blacksmiths of the Tuha-na-Anu on the special problems involved in the casting and weighting of a kind of hammer we have devised together. I hope to talk with you further this evening, Corum, when we all meet to debate our plans."

Corum raised his silver hand in a salute as the dwarf went down the steps and strode through a narrow street in the direction of the main gate.

For a moment Corum had the impulse to join Jhary, but it was most obvious that Jhary required no company at this time. After a while Corum, too, descended the steps, going in search of Medhbh, for suddenly he felt a great need to seek the consolation of the woman he loved.

It occurred to him as he made his way toward the king's hall that perhaps he was becoming too dependent upon the girl. Sometimes he felt that he needed her as another man might need drink or a drug. While she seemed to respond eagerly to this need, it could be that it was not fair to her to make the demands he did. As he walked to find her, he saw clearly that there were the seeds of considerable tragedy in the relationship which had developed between them. He shrugged. The seeds need not be nurtured. They could be destroyed. Even if his main destiny was pre-determined there were certain aspects of his personal life which he could control.

"Surely that must be so," he muttered to himself. A woman passing him on the street glanced at him, believing herself to be addressed. She was carrying a sheaf of staves which would be used for spears.

"My lord?"

"I observed that our preparations go well," Corum told her, embarrassed.

"Aye, my lord. We all work for the defeat of the Fhoi Myore." She shifted her load in her arms. "Thank you, my lord . . ."

"Aye." Corum nodded, hesitating. "Aye, good. Well, good morning to you."

"Good morning, my lord." She seemed amused.

Corum strode on, his head down, his lips firmly shut until he reached the hall of King Mannach, Medhbh's father.

But Medhbh was not there. A servant said to Corum: "She is at her weapons, Prince Corum, with some of the other women."

Prince Corum walked through a tunnel and into a high, wide chamber decorated with old battle flags and antique arms and armor, where a score of women practiced with bow, with spear, with sword and with sling. Medhbh herself was there, whirling her sling at a target at the far end of the chamber. She was famous for her skill with the sling and the tathlum, that awful missile made from the brains of a fallen enemy and thought to be of considerable supernatural effectiveness. As Corum entered, Medhbh let fly at the target and the tathlum struck it dead center, causing the thin bronze to ring and the target, which hung by a rope from the ceiling, to spin round and round, flashing in the light from the brands which helped light the chamber.

"Greetings," called Corum, his voice echoing, "Medhbh of the Long Arm!"

She turned, glad that he had witnessed her skill. "Greetings, Prince Corum." She dropped the sling and ran to him, embracing him, looking deep into his face. She frowned. "Are you melancholy, my love? What thoughts disturb you? Is there fresh news of the Fhoi Myore?"

28

"No." He held her to him, conscious that others of the women glanced at them. He said quietly: "I merely felt the need to see you."

She smiled tenderly back at him. "I am honored, Sidhi prince."

This particular choice of words, emphasizing the differences of blood and background between them, had the effect of disturbing him still more. He looked hard into her eyes and the look was not a kind one. She, recognizing this stare, looked surprised, taking a step back from him, her arms falling to her sides. He knew that he had failed in the purpose of his visit, for she, in turn, was disturbed. He had driven her from him. Yet had not she first created the alienation by her remark? For all that her smile had been tender, the phrase itself had somehow cut him. He turned away, saying distantly:

"Now that need is satisfied," he said; "I go to visit Ilbrec."

He wanted her to tell him to stay, but he knew she could not, no more than he could bear to remain. He left the hall without a further word.

And he cursed Jhary-a-Conel for introducing his gloomy thoughts into the day. He expected better of Jhary.

Yet, in fairness, he knew that too much was expected of Jhary and that Jhary had begun to resent it—if only momentarily—and he understood that he, Corum, was placing too much reliance on the strength of others and not enough upon himself. What right had he to demand such strength if he indulged his weaknesses?

"Eternal Champion I might be," he murmured, as he reached his own chambers, which he now shared with Medhbh, "but eternal pitier of myself, also, it sometimes seems."

And he lay down upon his bed and he considered his own character and at length he smiled and the mood began to leave him.

"It's obvious," he said. "Inaction suits me poorly and encourages the baser aspects of my character. My destiny is that of a warrior. Perhaps I should consider deeds and leave the question of thoughts to those better able to think." He laughed, then, becoming tolerant of his own weaknesses and resolving to indulge them no further.

Then he left his bed and went to find Ilbrec.

A RED SWORD IS LIFTED

Corum crossed the field, stepping over guy ropes and around the billowing walls of the tents on his way to Ilbrec's pavilion. He arrived, at last, outside the pavilion whose sea-blue silk rippled like little waves, and he called:

"Ilbrec! Son of Manannan, are you within?"

He was answered by a regular scraping noise which he was hard put, at first, to recognize, then he smiled, raising his voice:

"Ilbrec—I hear you preparing for battle. May I enter?"

The scraping noise ceased and the young giant's cheerful, booming voice replied:

"Enter, Corum. You are welcome."

Corum pushed aside the tent-flap. The only light within was the sunlight itself, piercing the silk, and giving the impression of a blue and watery cavern, not unlike part of Ilbrec's own domain beneath the waves. Ilbrec sat upon a great chest, his huge sword Retaliator across his knees. In his other hand was a whetstone with which he had been honing the sword. Ilbrec's golden hair hung in loose braids to his chest and today his beard was also plaited. He wore a simple green smock and sandals laced to his knees. In one corner of his tent lay his armor, his breastplate of bronze with its reliefs showing a great, stylized sun whose circle was filled with pictures of ships and of fish; his shield, which bore only the symbol of the sun; and his helmet, which had a similar motif. His lightly tanned arms had several heavy bracelets, both above and below the elbows; they were of gold and also matched the design of the breastplate. Ilbrec, son of the greatest of the Sidhi heroes, was a full sixteen feet high and perfectly proportioned.

Ilbrec grinned at Corum and began, again, to hone his sword.

"You look gloomy, friend."

Corum crossed the floor of the tent and stood beside Ilbrec's helmet, running his fleshly hand over the beautifully worked bronze. "Perhaps a premonition of my doom," he said.

"But you are immortal, are you not, Prince Corum?"

Corum turned at this new voice which was even younger in timber than Ilbrec's.

A youth of no more than fourteen summers had entered the tent. Corum recognized him as King Fiachadh's youngest son, called Young Fean by all. Young Fean resembled his father in looks, but his body was lithe where King Fiachadh's was burly and his features were delicate where his father's were heavy. His hair was as red as Fiachadh's and he had something of the same humor almost constantly in his eyes. He smiled at Corum, and Corum, as he always did, thought there was no creature in the world more charming than this young warrior who had already proved himself one of the cleverest and most proficient knights in all the company gathered here.

Corum laughed. "Possibly, Young Fean, aye. But somehow that thought does not console me."

Young Fean was sober for a moment, pushing back his light cloak of orange samite and removing his plain, steel helmet. He was sweating and had evidently just come from weapons practice. "I can understand that, Prince Corum." He made a slight bow in the direction of Ilbrec, who was plainly glad to see him. "Greetings to you, Lord Sidhi."

"Greetings, Young Fean. Is there some service I can do you?" Ilbrec continued to hone Retaliator with long, sweeping movements.

"None, I thank you. I merely came to talk." Young Fean hesitated, then replaced his helmet on his head. "But I see that I intrude."

"Not at all," said Corum. "How, in your opinion, do our men show."

"They are all good fighters. There is not one who is poor. But they are few, I think," said Young Fean.

"I agree with both your judgements," said Ilbrec. "I was considering the problem as I sat here."

"I have also discussed it," said Corum.

There was a long pause.

"But there is nowhere we can recruit more soldiers," said Young Fean, looking at Corum as if he hoped Corum would deny this statement.

"Nowhere at all," said Corum.

He noticed that Ilbrec said nothing and that the Sidhi giant was frowning.

"There is one place I heard of," said Ilbrec. "Long ago, when I was younger than Young Fean. A place where allies of the Sidhi might be found. But I heard, too, that it is a dangerous place, even for the Sidhi, and that the allies are fickle. I will consult with Goffanon later and ask him if he recalls more."

"Allies?" Young Fean laughed. "Supernatural allies? We have need of any allies, no matter how fickle."

"I will talk with Goffanon," said Ilbrec, and he returned to the honing of his sword.

Young Fean made to leave. "I will say nothing, then," he told them. "And I look forward to seeing you at the feast tonight."

When Young Fean had left Corum looked enquiringly at Ilbrec, but Ilbrec pretended an intense interest in honing his sword and would not meet Corum's eye.

Corum rubbed at his face. "I recall a time when I would have smiled at the very idea of magical forces at work in the world," he said.

Ilbrec nodded abstractedly, as if he did not really hear what Corum said.

"But now I have come to rely on such things." Corum's expression was ironic. "And must, perforce, believe in them. I heve lost my faith in logic and the power of reason."

Ilbrec looked up. "Perhaps your logic was too narrow and your reason limited, friend Corum?" he said quietly.

33

"Maybe." Corum sighed and moved to follow Young Fean through the tent-flap. Then, suddenly, he stopped short, putting his head on one side and listening hard. "Did you hear that sound?"

Ilbrec listened. "There are many sounds in the camp."

"I thought I heard the sound of a harp playing."

Ilbrec shook his head. "Pipes—in the distance—but no harp." Then he frowned, listening again. "Possibly, very faint, the strains of a harp. No." He laughed. "You are making me hear it, Corum."

But Corum knew he had heard the Dagdagh harp for a few moments and he was, again, troubled. He said nothing more of it to Ilbrec, but went out of the tent and across the field, hearing a distant voice crying his name:

"Corum! Corum!"

He turned. Behind him a group of kilted warriors were resting, sharing a bottle and conversing amongst themselves. Beyond these warriors Corum saw Medhbh running over the grass. It was Medhbh he had heard.

She ran round the group of warriors and stopped a foot or so from him, hesitantly stretching out her arm and touching his shoulder. "I sought you out in our chambers," she said softly, "but you had gone. We must not quarrel, Corum."

At once Corum's spirits lifted and he laughed and embraced her, careless of the warriors who had turned their attention upon the couple.

"We shall not quarrel again," he said. "Blame me, Medhbh."

"Blame no one. Blame nothing. Unless it be Fate." She kissed him. Her lips were warm. They were soft. He forgot his fears.

"What a great power women have," he said. "I have recently been speaking with Ilbrec of magic, but the greatest magic of all is in the kiss of a woman."

She pretended astonishment. "You become sentimental, Sir Sidhi."

And again, momentarily, he sensed that she withdrew

from him. Then she laughed and kissed him again. "Almost as sentimental as Medhbh!"

Hand in hand they wandered through the camp, waving to those they recognized or those who recognized them. At the edge of the camp several smithies had been set up. Furnaces roared as bellows forced their flames higher and higher. Hammers clanged on anvils. Huge, sweating men in aprons plunged iron into the fires and brought it out white and glowing and making the air shimmer. And in the center of all this activity was Goffanon, also in a great leathern apron, with a massive hammer in his hand, a pair of tongs in the other, deep in conversation with a black-bearded Mabden whom Corum recognized as the master smith Hisak, whose nickname was Sunthief, for it was said he stole the stuff of the sun itself and made bright weapons with it. In the nearby furnace a narrow piece of metal was immersed even now. Goffanon and Hisak watched this with considerable concentration as they talked and plainly it was this piece of metal they discussed.

Corum and Medhbh did not greet the two, but stood to one side and watched and listened.

"Six more heartbeats," they heard Hisak say, "and it will be ready."

Goffanon smiled. "Six and one-quarter heartbeats, believe me, Hisak."

"I believe you, Sidhi. I have learned to respect your wisdom and your skills."

Already Goffanon was extending his tongs into the fire. With a strange gentleness he gripped the metal and then swiftly withdrew it, his eye traveling up and down its length. "It is right," he said.

Hisak, too, inspected the white-hot metal, nodding. "It is right."

Goffanon's smile was almost ecstatic and he half turned, seeing Corum. "Aha, Prince Corum. You come at the perfect moment. See!" He lifted the strip of metal high. Now it glowed red hot, the color of fresh blood. "See, Corum! What do you see?"

"I see a sword blade."

"You see the finest sword blade made in Mabden lands. It has taken us a week to achieve this. Between us, Hisak and I have made it. It is a symbol of the old alliance between Mabden and Sidhi. Is it not fine?"

"It is very fine."

Goffanon swept the red sword back and forth through the air and the metal hummed. "It has yet to be fully tempered, but it is almost ready. It has yet to be given a name, but that will be left to you."

"To me?"

"Of course!" Goffanon laughed in delight. "Of course! It is your sword, Corum. It is the sword you will use when you lead the Mabden into battle."

"Mine?" Corum was taken aback.

"Our gift to you. Tonight, after the feast, we will return here and the sword will be ready for you. It will be a good friend to you, this sword, but only after you have named it will it be able to give you all its strength."

"I am honored, Goffanon," said Corum. "I had not guessed . . ."

The great dwarf tossed the blade into a trough of water and steam hissed. "Half of Sidhi manufacture, half of Mabden. The right sword for you, Corum."

"Indeed." Corum agreed. He was deeply moved by Goffanon's revelation. "Indeed, you are right, Goffanon." He turned to look shyly at the grinning Hisak. "I thank you, Hisak. I thank you both."

And then Goffanon said quietly and somewhat mysteriously: "It is not for nothing that Hisak is nicknamed the Sunthief. But still there is a song to be sung and a sign to be placed."

Respecting the rituals, but privately believing that they had no real significance, Corum nodded his head, convinced that an important honor had been done to him, but unable to define the exact nature of that honor.

"I thank you again," he said sincerely. "There are no words, for language is a poor thing which does no justice to the emotions I should like to express."

"Let there be no further words on this matter until the time comes for the sword-naming," said Hisak, speaking for the first time, his voice gruff and under-standing.

"I had come to consult you upon another matter," said Corum. "Ilbrec spoke of possible allies earlier. I wondered if this meant anything to you."

Goffanon shrugged. "I have already said that I can think of none."

"Then we will let the subject pass until Ilbrec has had time to speak to you himself," said Medhbh, touching Corum's sleeve. "We will see you tonight at the feast, my friends. Now we go to rest."

And she led a thoughtful Corum back toward the walls of Caer Mahlod.

AT THE FEAST

Now the great Hall of Caer Mahlod was filled. A stranger entering would not have guessed that the folk here prepared themselves for a final desperate war against an almost invincible foe; indeed the gathering seemed to have the spirit of a celebration. Four long oaken tables formed a hollow square in the center of which sat, not altogether comfortably, a golden-haired giant, Ilbrec, with his own beaker, plate and spoon set out before him. At the tables, facing inward, sat all the nobles of the Mabden, with the High King, slender, ascetic Amergin, in the place of greatest prominence, wearing his robe of silver thread and his crown of oak and holly leaves; Corum, with his embroidered eye-patch and his silver hand, was seated directly opposite the High King. On both sides of Amergin sat kings and beside the kings sat queens and princes and beside the princes sat princesses and great knights with their ladies. Corum had Medhbh on his right and Goffanon on his left, and beside Medhbh sat Jhary-a-Conel and beside Goffanon sat Hisak Sunthief the smith who had helped forge the unnamed blade. Rich silks and furs, garments of doeskin and plaid, ornaments of red gold and white silver, of polished iron and burnished bronze, of emerald and ruby and sapphire, brought blazing color to a hall lit by brightly burning brands of reeds soaked in oil. The air was full of smoke and the smell of food as whole beasts were roasted in the kitchens and brought quartered to the tables. Musicians, with harps and pipes and drums, sat in one corner playing sweet melodies which managed to blend with the voices of the company; the voices were cheerful and the conversation and the laughter were easy. The food was consumed lustily by all save Corum, who was in reasonable spirits but for some reason lacked an appetite. Exchanging a few words occasionally with

Goffanon or Jhary-a-Conel, sipping from a golden drinking horn, he glanced around him at the gathering, recognizing all the great heroes and heroines of the Mabden folk who were there. Apart from the five kings, King Mannach, King Fiachadh, King Daffyn, King Khonun of the Tuha-na-Anu and King Ghachbes of the Tuha-na-Tir-nam-Beo, there were many who had known glory and were already celebrated in the ballads of their people. Amongst these were Fionha and Cahleen, two daughters of the great dead knight Milgan the White, blonde-haired, creamy-skinned, almost twins, dressed in costumes of identical cut and color save that one was predominantly red, trimmed with blue and the other blue, trimmed with red, warrior maidens both, with honey-colored eyes and their hair all wild and unbound, flirting with a pair of knights a-piece; and nearby was the one called the Branch Hero, Phadrac-at-the-Crag-at-Lyth, almost as huge and as broad-shouldered as Goffanon, with green, glaring eyes and a red laughing mouth, whose weapon was a whole tree with which he would sweep his enemies from their horses and stun them. The Branch Hero laughed rarely, for he mourned his friend Ayan the Hairy-handed, whom he had killed during a mock fight when drunk. And at the next table was Young Fean, eating and drinking and flirting as heartily as any man, the darling of the nobles' daughters, who giggled at every word he said and stroked his red hair and fed him tidbits of meat and fruit. Near him sat all of the Five Knights of Eralskee, brothers who, until recent times, had refused to have aught to do with the folk of the Tuha-na-Anu for they had harbored a blood grudge against their uncle, King Khonun, whom they believed to be their father's murderer. For years they had remained in their mountains, venturing out to raid King Khonun's lands or to try to raise an army against him. Now they were sworn to forget their grudge until the matter of the Fhoi Myore was done. They were all similar in appearance, save that the youngest had black hair and an expression not quite as grim as that of his brothers, all sporting the high-peaked conical helmets bearing the Owl Crest of Eralskee, all big and very hard men who smiled as if the action were new to them. Then there was Morkyan of the Two Smiles, a scar on his face turning the lip on the left side upward and the lip on the right side downward; but this was not why he was called Morkyan of the Two Smiles. It was said that only Morkyan's enemies saw those two smiles—the first smile meant that he intended to kill them and the second smile meant that they were dead. Morkyan was splendid in dark blue leather and a matching leathern cap, his black beard trimmed to a point and his moustaches curling upward. He wore his hair short and hidden entirely by the tight-fitting cap. Leaning across two friends and speaking to Morkyan was Kernyn the Ragged who looked like a beggar and had impoverished himself through his strange habit of giving generous amounts of money to the kin of men he had slain. A demon in battle, Kernyn was always remorseful after he had killed an enemy and would make a point of finding the man's widow or family and bestowing a gift upon them. Kernyn's brown hair was matted and his beard was untidy. He wore a patched leather jerkin and a helmet of plain iron, and his long, mournful face was presently lit up as he regaled Morkyan with some reminiscence of a battle in which they had fought on different sides. Grynion Ox-rider was there, too, his arm around the ample waist of Sheonan the Axe-maiden, another woman of outstanding martial abilities. Grynion had earned his nickname for riding a wild ox into the thick of a fight when he had lost his horse and weapons and was wounded almost mortally. Helping himself from a huge side of beef, which he attacked with a large, sharp knife, was Ossan the Bridlemaker, renowned for his leather-working skill. His jerkin and his cap were made of embossed, finely-tooled hide, covered in a variety of flowing designs. He was a man nearing old age but his movements were those of a youth. He grinned as he forced meat into his mouth, the grease running into his ginger beard, and turned to listen to the knight who told a joke to those within hear-

ing of him. And there were many more: Fene the Leg-
less, Uther of the Melancholy Dale, Pwyll Spinebreaker,
Shamane the Tall and Shamane the Short, The Red Fox
Meyahn, Old Dylann, Ronan the Pale and Clar from
Beyond the West among them. Corum had met them all
as they had come to Caer Mahlod and he knew that
many of them would die when they battled, at last, with
the Fhoi Myore.

Now Amergin's clear, strong voice rang out, calling to
Corum:

"Well, Corum of the Silver Hand, are you satisfied
with the company you lead to war?"

Corum answered gracefully. "My only doubt is that
there are many here better able to lead such great warriors than I. It is my honor that I am elected to this task."

"Well-spoken!" King Fiachadh lifted his mead-horn.
"I toast Corum, the slayer of Sreng of the Seven Swords,
the savior of our High King. I toast Corum, who
brought back the Mabden pride!"

And Corum blushed as they cheered and drank his
health and when they had finished he stood up and
raised his own horn and he spoke these words:

"I toast that pride! I toast the Mabden folk!"

And again the company roared its approval and all
drank.

Then Amergin said:

"We are fortunate in having Sidhi allies who have
chosen to aid us in our struggle against the Fhoi Myore.
We are fortunate in that many of our great Treasures
were restored to us and used to defeat the Fhoi Myore
when they sought to destroy us. I toast the Sidhi and the
gifts of the Sidhi."

And again the whole company, save an embarrassed Ilbrec and a bemused Goffanon, drank and cheered.

Ilbrec was the next to speak. He said:

"If the Mabden were not courageous; if they were not
a fine-spirited folk, the Sidhi would not help them. We
fight for that which is noble in all living beings."

Goffanon grunted his agreement with this sentiment.

41

"By and large," he said, "the Mabden are not a selfish folk. They are not mean. They respect one another. They are not greedy. They are not, in the main, self-righteous. Aye, I've a liking for this people. I am glad that finally I chose to fight in their cause. It will be good to die in such a cause."

Amergin smiled. "I hope you do not expect death, Sir Goffanon. You speak of it as if it were an inevitable consequence of this venture."

And Goffanon lowered his eyes, shrugging.

King Mannach put in quickly: "We shall defeat the Fhoi Myore. We must. But I'll admit we could make use of any further advantages that Fate cares to send us." He looked meaningly at Corum who nodded.

"Magic is the best weapon against magic," he agreed, "if that is what you meant, King Mannach."

"It is what I meant," said Medhbh's father.

"Magic!" Goffanon laughed. "There's little of that left now, save the kind the Fhoi Myore and their friends can summon."

"Yet I heard of something . . ." Corum hardly realized he was speaking. He paused, reconsidering his impulse.

"Heard what?" said Amergin, leaning forward.

Corum looked at Ilbrec. "You spoke of a magical place, Ilbrec. Earlier today. You said you might know of somewhere where magical allies might be found."

Ilbrec glanced at Goffanon, who frowned. "I said I might know of such a place. It was a dim memory . . ."

"It is too dangerous," said Goffanon. "As I told you before, Ilbrec, I wonder at you suggesting it. We are best engaged in using to fullest advantage the resources we have now."

"Very well," said Ilbrec. "You were ever cautious, Goffanon."

"In this case rightly," grunted the Sidhi dwarf.

But now there was a silence in the hall as everyone listened to the exchange between the two Sidhi. Ilbrec looked about him, addressing all. "I made a mistake," he said. "Magic and such stuff has a habit of recoiling on those who use it."

"True," said Amergin. "We will respect your reserve, Sir Ilbrec."

"It is as well," said Ilbrec, but it was plain he did not really share Goffanon's caution. Caution was not part of the Sidhi youth's character, just as it had not been part of the great Manannan's nature.

"Your folk fought the Fhoi Myore in nine great fights," said King Fiachadh, wiping his mouth clean of the sticky mead which clung to it. "You know them best, therefore. And therefore we respect any advice you give us."

"And do you give us advice, Sir Sidhi?" Amergin asked.

Goffanon looked up from where he had been staring broodingly into his drinking beaker. His eyes were hard and sharp; they burned with a fire none had previously seen there. "Only that you should fear heroes," he said.

And no one asked him what he meant, for all were profoundly disturbed and perplexed by his remark.

At length King Mannach spoke. "It is agreed that we march directly for Caer Llud and make our first attack there. There are disadvantages to this plan—we go into the coldest of the Fhoi Myore territories—yet we have the chance of surprising them."

"Then we retreat again," said Corum. "Making the best speed we can for Craig Don, where we shall have left extra weapons, riding beasts, and food. From Craig Don we can make forays against the Fhoi Myore knowing that they will be unwilling to follow us through the seven circles. Our only danger will be if the Fhoi Myore are strong enough to hold Craig Don in siege until our food is gone."

"And that is why we must strike hard and strike swiftly at Caer Llud, taking as many of them as we can and conserving our own strength," said Morkyan of the Two Smiles, fingering his pointed beard. "There must be no displays of courage—no glory-deeds at Caer Llud."

His words were not particularly well-received by many in the company. "War-making is an art," said Kernyn the Ragged, his long face seeming to grow still longer, "though a terrible and immoral art. And most of us gathered here are artists, priding ourselves upon our skills—aye, and our style, too. If we cannot express ourselves in our individual ways, then is there any point to fighting at all?"

"Mabden fights are one thing," said Corum quietly, "but a war of Mabden against Fhoi Myore is another. There is more to lose than pride in the battles we contemplate tonight."

"I understand you," said Kernyn the Ragged, "but I am not sure I entirely agree with you, Sir Sidhi."

"We could give up too much in order to save our lives," said Sheonan the Axe-maiden, disengaging herself from Grynion's embrace.

"You spoke of what you admired in the Mabden." The Branch Hero, Phadrac, addressed Goffanon. "Yet there is a danger that we should sacrifice all the virtues of our folk merely in order to continue to exist."

"You must sacrifice nothing of that," Goffanon told him. "We merely counsel prudence during the assault on Caer Llud. One of the reasons that the Mabden lost so badly to the Fhoi Myore was because the Mabden warriors fight as individuals whereas the Fhoi Myore organize their forces as a single unit. At Caer Llud, if nowhere else, we must emulate these methods, using cavalry for fast-striking, using chariots as moving platforms from which to cast missiles. It would be pointless to stand and fight against Rhannon's horrible breath, would it not?"

"The Sidhi speak wisely," agreed Amergin, "and I beg all my folk to listen to them. That is why we are gathered here tonight, after all. I saw Caer Llud fall. I saw fine, brave war-knights fall before they could strike a single blow against their enemies. In the old times, in the times of the Nine Fights, Sidhi fought Fhoi Myore, one to one, but we are not Sidhi. We are Mabden. We must, in this instance, fight as a single folk."

The Branch Hero leant his great body backwards on the bench, nodding. "If Amergin decrees this, then I will fight as the Sidhi suggest. It is enough," he said.

And the others murmured their assent.

Now Ilbrec reached into his jerkin and drew out a rolled sheet of vellum. "Here," he said, "is a map of Caer Llud." He unrolled the sheet and turned, displaying it. "We attack simultaneously from four sides. Each force will be led by its king. This wall is considered the weakest and so two kings and their people will attack it. Ideally, we could move in to crush the Fhoi Myore and their slaves at the center of the city, but in actuality we shall probably not be successful in this and, having struck as hard as we can, will be forced to retreat, saving as many of our lives as possible for the second fight, at Craig Don . . ." And Ilbrec went on to explain the details of the plan.

Although one of those mainly responsible for the plan, Corum privately considered it over-optimistic, yet there was no better plan and so it would have to stand. He poured himself more mead from the pitcher at his elbow, passing the pitcher to Goffanon. Corum still wished that Goffanon had allowed Ilbrec to speak of the mysterious magical allies he considered too dangerous to enlist. As he accepted the pitcher, Goffanon said quietly: "We must leave here soon, for midnight approaches. The sword will be ready."

"There is little more to discuss," Corum agreed. "Let me know when you wish to go and I will make our excuses."

Now Ilbrec was answering the close questioning of some of the number who wished to hear how such and such a wall would be breached, and how long ordinary mortals might be expected to survive in the Fhoi Myore mist, and what kind of clothing would offer the best protection, and so on.

Seeing that he had no more to add to the discussion Corum stood up, courteously taking his leave of the High King and the rest of the gathering and, with

45

Medhbh, Goffanon and Hisak Sunthief beside him, strolled from the crowded hall into narrow streets and a cool night.

The sky was almost as light as day and the heavy buildings of the fortress-city were outlined blackly against it. A few pale, blue-tinted clouds flowed over the moon and onto the horizon, in the direction of the sea. They walked to the gate and crossed the bridge which spanned the moat, making their way round the edge of the camp and going toward the trees beyond. Somewhere a great owl hooted and there was the crack of wings, the squeal of a young rabbit. Insects chittered in the tall grass as they waded through it and entered the forest.

While the trees were still thin, Corum looked up into the clear sky, noting that once again, as it had been the last time he had entered this wood, the moon was full.

"Now," said Goffanon, "we go to the place of power where the sword awaits us."

And Corum found that he paused, reluctant to visit that mound where he had first entered this strange Mabden dream.

There came a sound from behind. Corum turned nervously, seeing, to his relief, that Jhary-a-Conel came to join them, his winged cat on his shoulder. Jhary grinned. "The hall was becoming too stuffy for Whiskers here." He stroked the cat's head. "I thought I might join you."

Goffanon seemed a trifle suspicious, but he nodded. "You are a welcome witness to what will transpire tonight, Jhary-a-Conel."

Jhary gave a bow. "I thank you."

Corum said: "Is there no other place we can go, Goffanon? Must it be Cremmsmound?"

"Cremmsmound is the nearest place of power," said Goffanon simply. "It would be too far to travel elsewhere."

Corum still did not move. He listened carefully to the sounds of the forest. "Do you hear the strains of a harp?" he asked.

"We are not close enough to the hall to hear the musicians," said Hisak Sunthief.

"You hear no harp in the wood?"

"I hear nothing," said Goffanon.

"Then I do not hear it," said Corum. "I thought for a moment it was the Dagdagh harp. The harp we heard when we summoned Oak Woman."

"An animal cry," said Medhbh.

"I fear that harp." Corum's voice was almost a whisper.

"There would be no need," Medhbh told him. "For the Dagdagh harp is wise. It is our friend."

Corum reached out and took her warm hand. "It is your friend, Medhbh of the Long Arm, but it is not mine. The old seeress told me to fear a harp, and that is the harp of which she spoke."

"Forget that prophecy. The old woman was plainly deranged. It was not a true prophecy." Medhbh stepped closer to him, her grip tightening. "You, of all of us, should not give in to superstition now, Corum."

Corum made a great effort and pushed the fear into the back of his mind. Then, momentarily, he met Jhary's eye. Jhary was troubled. He turned away, adjusting his wide-brimmed hat on his head.

"Now we must go quickly," growled Goffanon. "The time is near."

And, fighting off that morbid sense of doom, Corum followed the Sidhi dwarf deeper into the forest.

THE SWORD SONG OF THE SIDHI

It was as Corum had seen it before, Cremmsmound, with the white rays of the moon striking it, with the leaves of the oak trees shining like dark silver, all still. Corum studied the mound and wondered what lay beneath it. Did the mound really hide the bones of one who had been called Corum of the Silver Hand? And could those bones indeed be his own? The thought barely disturbed him at that moment. He watched Goffanon and Hisak Sunthief digging in the soft earth at the base of the mound, eventually drawing out a finished sword, a heavy, finely-tempered sword whose hilt was of plaited ribbons of iron. The sword seemed to attract the light of the moon and reflect it with increased brightness.

Careful not to touch the handle, holding the sword below the hilt, Goffanon inspected it, showing it to Hisak who nodded his approval.

"It will take much to dull the edge of this," said Goffanon. "Save for Ilbrec's sword Retaliator, there is no blade like it now in all the world."

"Is it steel?" Jhary-a-Conel stepped closer, peering at the sword. "It does not shine like steel."

"It is an alloy," said Hisak proudly. "Partly steel, partly Sidhi metal."

"I thought there was no Sidhi metal left upon this plane," Medhbh said. "I thought it all gone, save for that in Ilbrec's and Goffanon's weapons."

"It is what remains of an old Sidhi sword," said Goffanon. "Hisak had it. When we met he told me that he had kept it for many years, knowing no way in which to temper it. He got it from some miners who found it while they were digging for iron ore. It had been buried deep. I recognized it as one of a hundred swords I forged for the Sidhi before the Nine Fights. Only part of the blade remained. We shall never know how it came to be buried. Together Hisak and I conceived a way in which to blend the Sidhi metal with your Mabden metal and produce a sword containing the best properties of both."

Hisak Sunthief frowned. "And certain other properties, I understand."

"Possibly," said Goffanon. "We shall learn more in time."

"It is a fine sword," said Jhary, reaching toward it, "may I try it?"

But Goffanon withdrew it swiftly, almost nervously, shaking his head. "Only Corum," he said. "Only Corum."

"Then . . ." Corum made to take the sword. Goffanon raised his hand.

"Not yet," said the dwarf. "I have still to sing the song."

"Song?" Medhbh was curious.

"My sword song. A song was always sung at such a time as this." Goffanon lifted the sword toward the moon and it took on the aspect, for a moment, of a living thing; then it was a solid black cross framed against the great disc of the moon. "Each sword I make is different. Each must have a different song. Thus its identity is established. But I shall not name the blade. That task is Corum's. He must name the sword with the only name right for it. And when it is named, then the sword with fulfill its ultimate destiny."

"And what is that?" asked Corum.

Goffanon smiled. "I do not know. Only the sword will know."

"I thought you above such superstition, Sir Sidhi!" Jhary-a-Conel stroked his cat's neck.

"It is not superstition. It is something to do with an ability, at such times as these, to see into other planes, into other periods of time. What will happen will happen. Nothing we do here will change that, but we will have some *sense* of what is to come and that knowledge could be of use to us. I must sing my song, that is all I know." Goffanon looked defensive. Then he relaxed, turning his face to the moon. "You must listen and be silent while I sing."

"And what will you sing?" asked Medhbh.

"As yet," murmured Goffanon, "I do not know. My heart will tell me."

And, instinctively, they all fell back into the shadows of the oaks while Goffanon climbed slowly to the crest of Cremmsmound, the sword held by the blade in his two hands and lifted toward the moon. On the top of the mound he paused.

The night was full of heavy scents, of rustlings and the voices of small animals. The darkness in the surrounding grove was almost impenetrable. The oak trees were still. Then the sounds of the forest seemed to die away and Corum heard only the breathing of his companions.

For a long moment Goffanon neither moved nor spoke. His huge chest rose and fell rapidly and his eyes had closed. Then he moved slowly, lifting the sword to eight separate points before returning to his original position.

Then he began to sing. He sang in the beautiful, liquid speech of the Sidhi which was so like the Vadhagh tongue and which Corum could easily understand. This is what Goffanon sang:

> *Lo! I made the great swords*
> *Of a hundred Sidhi knights.*
> *Nine and ninety broke in battle.*
> *Only one came home.*
>
> *Some did rot in earth; some in ice;*
> *Some in trees; some under seas;*
> *Some melted in fire or were eaten.*
> *Only one came home.*
>
> *One blade, all broken, all torn,*
> *Of the Sidhi metal*
> *Not enough for a sword,*
> *So iron was added.*

50

> *Sidhi strength and Mabden strength*
>> *Combine in Goffanon's blade,*
> *His gift for Corum.*
>> *Weakness, too, this war-knife holds.*

Now Goffanon shifted his grip slightly upon the sword, raising it a little higher. He swayed, as one in a trance, before continuing:

> *Forged in fire, tempered in frost,*
>> *Power from the sun, wisdom from the moon,*
> *Fine and fallible,*
>> *This brand is fated.*

> *Ah! They will hate it,*
>> *Those ghosts of the yet-to-come!*
> *Even now the sword thirsts for them.*
>> *Their blood grows chill.*

And it seemed almost that Goffanon balanced the blade by its tip and that it stood upright under its own volition.

(And Corum recalled a dream and he recoiled. When had he handled such a sword before?)

> *Soon will come the naming,*
>> *Then the foe shall shudder!*
> *Here is a handsome needle,*
>> *To stitch the Fhoi Myore shroud!*

> *Glaive! Goffanon made thee!*
>> *Now you go to Corum!*
> *Worms and carrion eaters*
>> *Will call you 'Friend.'*

> *Harsh shall be the slaughter,*
>> *Ere the winter's vanquished,*
> *Good, red reaping*
>> *For a Sidhi scythe!*

> Then must come the naming;
> Then must come the tally.
> Sidhi and Vadhagh both shall
> Pay the score.

Now a frightful shuddering possessed Goffanon's bulky body and he came close to losing his grip on the sword.

Corum wondered why the others did not seem to hear Goffanon when he groaned. He looked at their faces. They stood entranced, uncomprehending, over-awed.

Goffanon hesitated, rallied himself, and went on:

> Unnamed blade, I call thee Corum's sword!
> Hisak and Goffanon claim thee not!
> Black winds cry through Limbo!
> Blind rivers await my soul!

These last words Goffanon screamed. He appeared terrified by what he saw through his closed eyes, but his sword-song still issued from his bearded lips.

(Had Corum ever seen this sword? No. But there had been another like it. This sword would prove useful against the Fhoi Myore, he knew. But was the sword really a friend? Why did he consider it an enemy?)

> This was a fated forging;
> But now that it is done
> The blade, like its destiny,
> Cannot be broken.

Corum could see only the sword. He found that he was moving toward it, climbing the mound. It was as if Goffanon had disappeared and the blade hung in the air, burning sometimes white like the moon, sometimes red like the sun.

Corum reached out for the handle with his silver fingers, but the sword seemed to retreat. Only when Corum stretched his left hand, his hand of flesh, toward it did it allow him to approach.

52

Corum still heard Goffanon's song. The song had begun as a proud chant; now it was a melancholy dirge. And was the dirge accompanied, in the far distance, by the strains of a harp?

> Here is a fitting sword,
>   Half mortal, half immortal,
> For the Vadhagh hero.
>   Here is Corum's sword.

> There is no comfort in the blade I made,
>   It was forged for more than war;
> It will kill more than flesh;
>   It will grant both more and less than death.

> Fly, blade! Rush to Corum's grip!
>   Forget Goffanon made thee!
> Doom only the Mabden's foes!
>   Learn loyalty, shun treachery!

And suddenly the sword was in Corum's left hand and it was as if he had known such a sword all his life. It fitted his grasp perfectly; its balance was superb. He turned it this way and that in the light of the moon, wondering at its sharpness and its handling.

"It is my sword," he said. He felt that he was united with something he had lost long since and then forgotten about.

"It is my sword."

> Serve well the knight who knoweth thee!

Abruptly, Goffanon's song ended. The great dwarf's eyes opened; his expression was a mixture of tormented guilt, sympathy for Corum, and triumph. Then Goffanon turned to peer at the moon. Corum followed his gaze and was transfixed by the great silver disc which apparently filled the whole sky. Corum felt as though he were being drawn into the moon. He saw faces there, scenes of fighting armies, wastelands, ruined cities and fields. He saw himself, though the face was not his. He saw a sword not unlike the one he now held, but the other sword was black, whereas his was white. He saw Jhary-a-Conel. He saw Medhbh. He saw Rhalina and he saw other women, and he loved them all, but of Medhbh alone he felt fear. Then the Dagdagh Harp appeared and changed into the form of a youth whose body shone with a strange golden color and who, in some way, was also the harp. Then he saw a great, pale horse and he knew that the horse was his but he was wary of where the horse would take him. Then Corum saw a plain all white with snow and across this plain came a single rider whose robe was scarlet and whose arms and armor were those of the Vadhagh and who had one hand of flesh and one of metal and whose right eye was covered by an elaborately embroidered patch and whose features were the features of a Vadhagh, of Corum. And Corum knew that this rider was not himself and he gasped in terror and tried not to look as the rider came closer and closer, an expression of mocking hatred upon his face and in his single eye the unequivocal determination to kill Corum and take his place.

"No!" cried Corum.

And clouds moved across the moon and the light dimmed and Corum stood upon Cremmsmound in the oak grove, the place of power, with a sword in his hand that was unlike any sword forged before this day; and Corum looked down the mound and saw that Goffanon now stood with Hisak Sunthief and Jhary-a-Conel and Medhbh the red-haired, Medhbh of the Long Arm, and all four stared at Corum as if they wished to help him and could not.

Corum did not know why he replied to their expressions in the way he did when he raised the sword high over his head and said to them in a quiet, firm voice:

"I am Corum. This is my sword. I am alone."

Then the four walked up the mound and they took him back to Caer Mahlod where many still feasted, unaware of what had taken place in the oak grove when the moon had been at its fullest.

The Fifth Chapter

A COMPANY OF HORSEMEN

Corum slept long into the following morning, but it was not a dreamless sleep. Voices spoke to him of untrustworthy heroes and noble traitors; he had visions of swords, both the one he had been given during the ceremony in the oak grove and others, in particular one other, a black blade which seemed, like the Dagdagh Harp, to have a complex personality, as if inhabited by the spirit of a particularly powerful demon. And between hearing these voices and seeing these visions he heard the words repeated over and over again:

"You are the Champion. You are the Champion."

And sometimes a chorus of voices would tell him:

"You must follow the Champion's Way."

And what, he would wonder, if that way were not the way of the Mabden whom he had sworn to help?

And the chorus would repeat:

"You must follow the Champion's Way."

And Corum awoke, eventually, saying aloud:

"I have no liking for this dream."

He spoke of the dream into which he had awakened.

Medhbh, dressed, fresh-faced and determined, was standing beside the bed. "What dream is that, my love?"

He shrugged and tried to smile. "Nothing. Last night's events disturbed me, I suppose." He looked into her eyes and he felt a little fear creep into his mind. He reached out and took hold of her soft hands, her strong, cool hands. "Do you really love me, Medhbh?"

She was disconcerted. "I do," she said.

He looked beyond her to the carved chest on the lid of which rested the sword Goffanon had given him. "How shall I name the sword?"

She smiled. "You will know. Is that not what Goffanon

told you? You will know what to call it when the time comes and then the sword will be informed with all its powers."

He sat up, the covers falling away from his broad, naked chest.

She went to the far side of the chamber and signalled to someone in the next room. "Prince Corum's bath. Is it ready?"

"It is ready, my lady."

"Come, Corum," said Medhbh. "Refresh yourself. Wash away your unpleasant dreams. In two days we shall be ready to march. There is little left for you to do until then. Let us spend those two days as enjoyably as we can. Let us ride, this morning, beyond the woods and over the moors."

He drew a deep breath. "Aye," he said lightly. "I am a fool to brood. If my destiny is set, then it is set."

Amergin met them as they mounted their horses an hour later. Amergin was tall, slender and youthful but had the dignity of a man much older than he looked. He wore the blue and gold robes of the Archdruid and there was a simple coronet of iron and raw gems set upon his head of long, fair hair.

"Greetings," said the High King. "Did your business go well last night, Prince Corum?"

"I think so," said Corum. "Goffanon seemed satisfied."

"But you do not carry the sword he gave you."

"It is not a sword, I think, to be worn casually." Corum had his old, good sword at his side. "I shall carry Goffanon's gift into battle, however."

Amergin nodded. He looked down at the cobbles of the courtyard, apparently in deep thought. "Goffanon told you no more of those allies Ilbrec mentioned."

"I took it that Goffanon did not regard them, whoever they are, as allies, necessarily," said Medhbh.

"Just so," said Amergin. "However, it would seem to me it would be worth risking much if it meant that our chances of defeating the Fhoi Myore were improved."

Corum was surprised by what he guessed to be the import of Amergin's words. "You do not think we shall be successful?"

"The attack on Caer Llud will cost us dear," said Amergin quietly. "I meditated on our plan last night. I believe I had a vision."

"Of defeat?"

"It was not a vision of victory. You know Caer Llud, Corum, as do I. You know how utterly cold it is now that the Fhoi Myore inhabit it. Cold of that order affects men often in ways they do not fully comprehend."

"That is true." Corum nodded.

"That is all that I thought," said Amergin. "A simple thought. I cannot be more specific."

"You do not need to be, High King. But I fear there is no better means of making war against our enemies. If there were . . ."

"We should all know it." Amergin shrugged and patted the neck of Corum's horse. "But if you have the opportunity to reason with Goffanon again, beg him at very least to tell us the nature of these allies."

"I promise you that I shall, Archdruid, but I do not anticipate any success."

"No," said Amergin, his hand falling away from the horse. "Neither do I."

They rode out from Caer Mahlod, leaving behind them a thoughtful Archdruid, and soon they were galloping through the oak woods and up into the high moorlands where curlews rose and sank above their heads and the smell of the bracken and the heather was sweet in their nostrils and it seemed that no power in the universe could change the simple beauties of the landscape. The sun was warm in a soft blue sky. It was a kindly day. And soon their spirits had risen higher than ever before and they dismounted from their horses and wandered through the knee-high bracken and then sank down into it so that all they could see was the sky and the cool, restful green of the ferns on all sides. And they held each other and they made gentle love then lay close together in silence, breathing the good air and listening to the quiet sounds of the moorlands.

They were allowed an hour of this peace before Corum detected a faint pulsing from the ground beneath him and put his ear to the source, knowing what it must mean.

"Horses," he said, "coming nearer."

"Fhoi Myore riders?" She sat up, reaching for her sling and her pouch which she carried everywhere.

"Perhaps. Gaynor, or the People of the Pines, or both. Yet we have outriders everywhere at present to warn us of an attack from the east and we know that all the Fhoi Myore gather in the east at present." Cautiously he began to raise his head. The horsemen were coming from the northwest, more or less from the direction of the coast. His view was blocked by the rise of a hill, but now, very faintly, he thought he could hear the jingle of harness. Looking behind him, Corum could see that their horses would be clearly visible to anyone approaching over that hill. He drew his sword and began to creep towards the horses. Medhbh followed him.

Hastily, they clambered into their saddles, riding toward the hill, but at an angle to the approaching horsemen, so that, with luck, they would not immediately be seen if they crested the hill.

An outcrop of white limestone offered them some cover and they drew rein behind this, waiting until the riders came in sight.

Almost immediately the first three appeared. The ponies they rode were small and shaggy and dwarfed by the size of the broad-shouldered men on their backs. These men all had the same blazing pale red hair and sharp blue eyes. The hair of their beards was plaited into a dozen narrow braids and the hair of their heads hung in four or five very thick braids into which were bound strands of beads, glinting in the sunlight. They had long oval shields strapped to their left arms and these shields appeared to be of hide and wicker reinforced with rims and bands of brass hammered into bold, flowing designs.

The shields appeared to have sheaths attached to their inner surfaces and into these were stuck two iron-headed spears shod with brass. On their hips the men sported short, wide-bladed swords in leather, iron-studded sheaths. Some wore their helmets and others carried them over their saddle pommels and the helmets were all roughly of the same design: conical caps of leather ribbed by iron or brass and decorated with the long, curving horns of the mountain ox. In some cases the original horn had been completely obscured by the polished pebbles, bits of iron or brass or even gold, set into it. Thick plaid cloaks predominantly of red, blue or green were flung over their shoulders. They had kilts either of plaid or of leather and their legs were naked; only a few wore any kind of footgear and of these most wore a simple sandal strapped at the ankle. They were, without doubt, warriors, but Corum had seen none quite like these, though to a degree they resembled the folk of Tir-nam-Beo and the ponies reminded him of those ridden by his old enemies of the forests near Moidel's Mount. Eventually all the riders came into sight—about a score of them—and as they rode closer it was evident they had lately experienced hardship. Some had broken limbs, others had wounds bound up and two of the men were strapped tightly to their saddles so that they would not fall from their horses.

"I do not think they mean harm to Caer Mahlod," said Medhbh. "These are Mabden. But what Mabden? I thought all warriors had been summoned by now."

"They have traveled far and hard by the look of them," murmured Corum. "And over the sea, too. Look, their cloaks bear the stains of sea-water. Perhaps they have left a boat near here. Come, let us hail them." He urged his horse from its cover behind the limestone crag, calling out to the newcomers:

"I bid you good afternoon, strangers. Where are you bound?"

The burly warrior in the vanguard reined in his pony suddenly, his red brows coming together in a suspicious scowl, his heavy, gnarled hand reaching toward the handle of his sword, and when he spoke his tone was deep and coarse.

"I bid you a good afternoon, also," he said, "if you mean us no harm. As for where we are bound, well, that is our business."

"It is also the business of those whose land this is," Corum answered reasonably.

"That could be," the warrior answered. "But if it be not Mabden land, then you have conquered it and if you have conquered it, then you are our enemy and we must slay you. We can see that you are not Mabden."

"True. But I serve the Mabden cause. And this lady, she is Mabden."

"She resembles a Mabden, certainly," said the warrior, dropping none of his caution. "But we have seen too many illusions on our journey here to be deceived by what is apparently so."

"I am Medhbh," said Medhbh fiercely, offended. "I am Medhbh of the Long Arm, famous in my own right as a warrior. And I am the daughter of King Mannach, who rules this land from Caer Mahlod."

The warrior became a trifle less suspicious, but he kept his hand upon the hilt of his sword and the others spread out as if they prepared to attack Medhbh and Corum.

"And I am Corum," said Corum, "once called the Prince in the Scarlet Robe, but I traded that robe to a wizard and now I am called Corum of the Silver Hand." He held up his metal hand which, up to that point, he had concealed. "Have you not heard of me? I fight for the Mabden against the Fhoi Myore."

"That is he!" One of the younger warriors behind the leader shouted and pointed at Corum. "The scarlet robe —he does not wear it now—but the features are the same—the eye-patch is the same. That is he!"

"You have followed us, then, Sir Demon," said the leading warrior. He sighed, turned in his saddle and looked back at his men. "These are all that are left, but

60

perhaps we can defeat you and your she-demon consort."

"He is no demon and neither am I!" cried Medhbh angrily. "Why do you accuse us of this? Where have you seen us before?"

"We have not seen you before," said the leader. He steadied his nervous pony with a movement of the reins. His harness clattered and his metal stirrup struck the rim of his long shield. "We have seen only this one." He nodded at Corum. "In those foul and sorcerous islands back there." He jerked his head in the direction of the sea. "The island where we beached eight good longships and ten rafts of provisions and livestock, going ashore for fresh water and meat. You will recall," he continued, staring with hatred at Corum, "that when we left it was with but a single ship, no women or children, no livestock save our ponies, and few provisions."

Corum said: "I assure you that you have not seen me until this moment. I am Corum. I fight the Fhoi Myore. These last weeks I have spent at Caer Mahlod. I have not left at any time. This is the first journey I have taken beyond the immediate confines of the city in a month!"

"You are the one who came against us on the island," said the youth who had first accused Corum. "In your red cloak, with your helmet of mock-silver, with your face all pale like that of a dead thing, with your eye-patch and your laughter . . ."

"A Shefanhow," said the leader. "We know you."

"It has been literally a lifetime since I heard that word used," said Corum sombrely. "You are close to angering me, stranger. I speak the truth. You must have come to blows with an enemy who resembled me in some way."

"Aye!" the youth laughed bitterly. "To the extent of being your twin! We feared you would follow us. But we are ready to defend ourselves against you. Where do your men hide?" He looked about him, his braids swinging with the movement of his head.

"I have no men," said Corum impatiently.

The leader laughed harshly. "Then you are foolish."

61

"I will not fight you," Corum told him. "Why are you here?"

"To join those who gather at Caer Mahlod."

"It is as I thought." All Corum's earlier forebodings had returned and he fought to hold them off. "If we give you our weapons and take you to Caer Mahlod, will you believe that we mean you no harm? At Caer Mahlod you will learn that we speak the truth, that we have never seen you before and that we are not your enemies."

The loud-voiced youth called: "It could be a trick, to lure us into a trap."

"Ride with your swords at our throats if you like," said Corum carelessly. "If you are attacked, you may kill us."

The leader frowned. "You have none of the manner of that other we met on the island," he said. "And if you lead us to Caer Mahlod at least we shall have reached our destination and thus gained something from this meeting."

"Artek!" shouted the youth. "Be wary!"

The leader turned. "Silence, Kawanh. We can always slay the Shefanhow later!"

"I would ask you, in courtesy," said Corum evenly, "not to employ that term when you refer to me. It is not one I like and it does not make me sympathetic to you."

Artek made to answer, a hard smile half-forming on his lips. Then he looked into Corum's single eye and thought better of his reply. He grunted and ordered two of his men forward. "Take their weapons. Hold your swords at them as we ride. Very well—Corum—lead us to Caer Mahlod."

Corum derived some pleasure from the looks of shock on the strangers' faces as they rode to the outskirts of the camp and saw the expressions of concern and anger in the eyes of every Mabden who became aware that Corum and Medhbh were prisoners. Now it was Corum's turn to smile and his smile was broad as the crowd around the twenty riders became thicker and thicker until they were no longer able to advance and came to a halt in the middle of the camp, still some distance from the hill on which Caer Mahlod was built. A war-chief of the Tirnam-Beo glared at Artek, whose sword pressed upon Corum's chest.

"What mean you by this, man! Why do you hold hostage our princess? Why threaten the life of our friend, Prince Corum?"

Artek's embarrassment was so complete that he blushed a deeper red than his hair and beard. "So you spoke the truth . . ." he muttered. But he did not lower his sword. "Unless this is some monstrous illusion and all these are your demon followers."

Corum shrugged. "If they are demons, Sir Artek, then you are doomed, anyway, are you not?"

Miserably Artek sheathed his sword. "You are right. I must believe you. Yet your resemblance to the one who attacked us on that hateful and haunted isle is so close—you would not blame me, Prince Corum, if you saw him."

Corum answered so that only Artek could hear. "I think that I have seen him—in a dream. Later, Sir Artek, you and I must talk about this, for I believe the evil which was worked against you will soon be directed against me—and the results could be even more tragic."

Artek darted him a puzzled glance but, respecting the tone of Corum's words, said nothing further.

"You must rest and you must eat," said Corum. He had taken a liking to the barbarian in spite of the poor circumstances of their meeting. "Then you must tell us all your tale in the great hall of Caer Mahlod."

Artek bowed. "You are generous, Prince Corum, and you are courteous. Now I see why the Mabden respect you."

CONCERNING THE VOYAGE OF THE PEOPLE OF FYEAN

"We are an island folk," said Artek, "living mainly off the sea. We fish—" he paused—"well, in the past, until recently, we—well, we were sea-raiders, in short. It is a hard life on our islands. Little grows there. Sometimes we raided nearby coasts, at other times we attacked ships and took what we needed to survive . . ."

"I know you now." King Fiachadh laughed heartily. "You are pirates, are you not! You are Artek of Clonghar. Why the folk of our sea ports pass water at the very mention of your name!"

Artek made a feeble gesture and again he blushed. "I am that same Artek," he admitted.

"Fear not, Artek of Clonghar," smiled King Mannach, leaning across the table and patting the pirate upon the hand, "all old scores are forgotten in Caer Mahlod. Here we have only one enemy—the Fhoi Myore. Tell us how you came here."

"One of the ships we raided was from Gwyddneu Garanhir—on its way to Tir-nam-Beo, we discovered, with a message for the king of that land. From that ship we learned of the great massing against the Fhoi Myore. While we have never encountered this folk—living in the remote northwest as we do—we felt that if all the Mabden were joining together against the Cold Folk then we should help also—that their fight was our fight in this case." He grinned, recovering some of his buoyancy. "Besides—without your ships, how should *we* live? So it was in our interest to ensure that you survived. We readied all our own boats—more than a score—and built strong, water-tight rafts to tow behind them, taking all our folk from Fyean—our whole island's name—since we did not wish to leave our women and children unprotected." Artek stopped, lowering his eyes. "Ah, how I wish we had left them. Then, at least, they might have died in their own homes and not on the shifting shores of that terrible island."

Ilbrec, who had squeezed himself into the hall to hear Artek's story, said quietly: "Where is this island?"

"A little to the north and west of Clonghar. The storm drove us in that direction. During the same storm we lost most of our water and much of our meat. Do you know the place, Sir Sidhi?"

"Has it a single high hill, very even in its proportions, at its center?"

Artek inclined his head. "It has."

"And does one huge pine tree grow on the peak of that hill at the exact center?"

"There is the biggest pine I have ever seen there," agreed Artek.

"When you have landed does everything seem to shimmer and threaten to change its appearance, save for that hill which remains sharp and solid in outline?"

"You have been there!" said Artek.

"No," said Ilbrec. "I have only heard of the place." And he darted a very hard stare at Goffanon, who affected to be without interest in this island and looked studiously bored. But Corum knew the dwarf well enough to see that Goffanon was deliberately ignoring the import of Ilbrec's glance.

"We sea-warriors have passed the island before, of course, but since it is often surrounded by mist and there are hidden rocks at various points off its coast, we have never actually landed there. We have never had the necessity to do so."

"Though some have been thought shipwrecked there in the past and never found," added the eager youth Kawanh. "There are superstitions about the place—that it is inhabited by Shefanhow and such . . ." His voice trailed off.

"Is it sometimes called Ynys Scaith, this place?" asked Ilbrec, still thoughtful.

"I have heard it called that, aye," Artek agreed. "It is an old, old name for the place."

"So you have been to Shadow Island." Ilbrec shook his fair head, half amused. "Fate draws at more threads than we guessed, eh, Goffanon?"

But Goffanon pretended that he had not heard Ilbrec, though later Corum saw him offer his fellow Sidhi a secret, warning glare.

"Aye and that is where we saw Prince Corum here—or his double—" blurted Kawanh, then stopped. "I apologise, Prince Corum," he said. "I had not meant . . ."

Corum smiled. "Perhaps it was my shadow you saw. After all, the place is called Ynys Scaith—the Isle of Shadows. An evil shadow, however." The smile faded on his face.

"I have heard of Ynys Scaith." Until this moment Amergin had said nothing beyond a formal greeting to Artek and his men. "A place of dark sorcery where evil druids would go to work their magic. A place shunned even by the Sidhi . . ." And now it was Amergin's turn to look meaningfully at both Ilbrec and Goffanon, and Corum guessed that the wise Archdruid had also noticed the exchange of glances between the two Sidhi. "Ynys Scaith, so I was taught as a novice, existed even before the coming of the Sidhi. It shares certain properties with the Sidhi isle of Hy-Breasail, but is in other ways unlike that place. Where Hy-Breasail was supposed to be a land of fair enchantments, Ynys Scaith was said to be an island of black madness . . ."

"Aye," growled Goffanon. "It is, to say the least, inhospitable to Sidhi and Mabden alike."

"You have been there, Goffanon?" Amergin asked gently.

But Goffanon had become wary again. "Once," he said.

"Black madness and red despair," put in Artek. "When we landed there we found ourselves unable to return to our ships. Disgusting forests grew up in our path. Mists engulfed us. Demons attacked us. All kinds of misshapen beasts lurked in wait for us. They destroyed all our children. They slew all our women and most of our

66

menfolk. We are the only ones, of the whole race of Fyean, who survived—and that by luck, stumbling accidentally upon one of our ships and sailing directly for your shores." Artek shuddered. "Even if I knew my wife was still alive and trapped upon Ynys Scaith I would not return." Artek clenched his two hands together. "I could not."

"She is dead," said Kawanh gently. He was comforting his leader. "I saw it happen."

"How could we be sure that what we saw was in any way reality!" Artek's eyes filled with agony.

"No," said Kawanh. "She is dead, Artek."

"Aye," Artek's hands parted. His shoulders slumped. "She is dead."

"Now you know why I would have no part of your idea," murmured Goffanon to Ilbrec.

Corum looked away from the still shaking Artek of Clonghar. He looked at the two Sidhi. "Is that where you thought we should find allies, Ilbrec?"

Ilbrec motioned with his hand, dismissing his own idea. "It was."

"Nothing but evil comes from Ynys Scaith," Goffanon said. "Only evil, no matter how disguised."

"I had not realized . . ." Amergin reached out and touched Artek upon the shoulder. "Artek, I will give you a potion that will make you sleep and will ensure that you will not dream. In the morning you will be a man again."

The sun was setting over the camp. Ilbrec and Corum walked toward the Sidhi's blue tent. From a score of cooking fires came the mingled smells of a variety of meals. Nearby a boy sang of heroes and great deeds in a high, melancholy voice. They entered the tent.

"Poor Artek," said Corum. "What allies had you hoped to find on Ynys Scaith?"

Ilbrec shrugged. "Oh, I thought that the inhabitants—certain of them, at least, might be bribed to side with us.

I suppose that my judgement was poor, as Goffanon said."

"Artek and his followers thought they saw me there," Corum told him. "They thought I was one of those who slew their companions."

"That puzzles me," said Ilbrec. "I have heard of nothing like that before. Perhaps you do have a twin . . . Did you ever have a brother?"

"A brother?" Corum was reminded of the old woman's prophecy. "No. But I was warned to fear one. I thought the warning might apply to Gaynor who, spiritually in some ways, is a brother. Or whoever it is lying under the hill in the oak grove. But now I think that brother awaits me in Ynys Scaith."

"Awaits you?" Ilbrec was alarmed. "You do not mean to visit the Isle of Shadows?"

"It occurred to me that those powerful enough to destroy the best part of the people of Fyean, fearsome enough to terrify one as brave as Artek, would be good allies to have," said Corum. "Besides, I would face this 'brother' and discover who he is and why I should fear him."

"It is unlikely that you would survive the dangers of Ynys Scaith," mused Ilbrec, seating himself in his great chair and drumming his fingers upon his table.

"I am in a mood to take most risks with my own destiny," said Corum softly, "so long as it is not to the disadvantage to these Mabden we serve."

"I, too." Ilbrec's sea-blue eyes met Corum's eye. "But the Mabden march to Caer Llud the day after tomorrow and you must lead them in their war."

"That is what stops me from sailing immediately to Ynys Scaith," said Corum. "That is all."

"You fear not for your own life—your sanity—perhaps your soul?"

"I am called Champion Eternal. What is death, or madness to me, who shall live many more lives than this? How can my soul be trapped if it is needed elsewhere? If anyone has the chance of visiting Ynys Scaith and returning, then surely it is Corum of the Silver Hand?"

"Your logic has flaws," said Ilbrec. He looked broodingly into the middle-distance. "But you are right in one point—you are the best-fitted to seek Ynys Scaith."

"And there I could attempt to employ its inhabitants in our service."

"They would be of great use to us," admitted Ilbrec. Cold air came into the tent as the flap parted. Goffanon stood there, his axe upon his shoulder. "Good evening, my friends," he said.

They greeted him. He sat himself down on Ilbrec's war-chest, placing his axe carefully beside him. He looked from Corum to Ilbrec and back again. He read something in both their faces that disturbed him. "Well," he said, "I hope you heard enough just now to dissuade you from the foolhardy scheme Ilbrec was considering earlier."

"You planned to go there?" Corum asked.

Ilbrec spread his hands. "I had thought . . ."

"I have been there," interrupted Goffanon. "That was my bad luck. My good luck was that I managed to escape. Evil druids used that island before the Mabden grew to power on this plane. It existed as a place before the rising of the Vadhagh and the Nhadragh, even— though it was not then on this plane."

"Then how came it here?" asked Corum.

Ilbrec cleared his throat. "An accident. For some reason there were those who grew powerful enough in its own plane to be able to destroy it. As fate would have it this was at the time when we Sidhi were coming through to help the Mabden against the Fhoi Myore. The inhabitants of Ynys Scaith were able to break through to this plane under cover of our own movements so, indirectly, the Sidhi are responsible for that place of horror existing here. Thus Ynys Scaith escaped the vengeance of the people of its own world, yet I heard that this world is inhospitable to them—they cannot leave their island without certain aids or they inevitably die. They seek a means of returning to their own plane or some other more hospitable to them. Thus far they have been unsuccessful.

That is why I thought we might bargain with them to come to our aid—if we offered to help them."

"They would betray us, no matter what bargain they made with us," Goffanon said. "It is as much in their nature to do so as it is in our nature to breath air."

"We should have to guard against such a happening," said Ilbrec.

Goffanon gestured impatiently. "We could not. Listen to me, Ilbrec! Once I had the notion to visit Ynys Scaith, during the quiet times following the defeat of the Fhoi Myore. I knew what the Mabden said of Hy-Breasail, my own home—that it was inhabited by demons. I thought, therefore, that probably Ynys Scaith was a similar place —that while Mabden perished there, Sidhi would survive. I was wrong. What Hy-Breasail is to the Mabden, so Ynys Scaith is to the Sidhi. It belongs neither to this plane nor to ours. Moreover, the inhabitants use the properties of their land deliberately to torture and to slay all visitors not of their own kind."

"Yet you escaped," put in Corum. "And Artek and a few others survived."

"By luck in both cases. Artek told you that they found their ship by purest chance. Similarly, I stumbled into the sea. Once clear of Ynys Scaith I could not be followed by the inhabitants. I swam for more than a day before I reached an island little more than a crag of rock jutting from the sea. There I remained until sighted by a ship. They were wary of me, but they took me aboard and eventually I made my way back to Hy-Breasail and never left thereafter."

"You mentioned nothing of this when first we met," said Corum.

"For good reason," growled the Sidhi smith. "I would have mentioned nothing now, save that Artek spoke of it."

"Yet you speak only of general terrors, not of specific dangers," said Ilbrec reasonably.

"That," said Goffanon, "is because the specific dangers are indescribable." He got up. "We fight the Fhoi Myore without seeking such allies as the folk of Ynys

Scaith. That way some of us might survive. The other way—we are all doomed. I speak the truth."

"As you see it," Corum could not resist saying.

At this, Goffanon's face hardened. He picked up his axe, flung it onto his shoulder and left the tent without another word.

The Seventh Chapter

IN WHICH OLD FRIENDSHIPS APPEAR SUD-
DENLY DISCARDED

Amergin came to Corum's chambers that night while Medhbh was elsewhere, visiting her father. He entered without knocking and Corum, who had been staring through the window at the fires of the camp, turned when he detected a footfall.

Amergin spread his thin hands. "I apologise for my rudeness, Prince Corum, but I wished to speak with you privately. I gather that you have angered Goffanon in some way."

Corum nodded. "There was a dispute."

"Concerning Ynys Scaith?"

"Aye."

"You had considered visiting the place?"

"I am due to lead your army on the day after tomorrow. Clearly it would be impossible for me to do both." Corum indicated a carved chair. "Be seated, Archdruid."

Corum sat down upon his bed as Amergin lowered himself into the chair.

"Yet you would go, if you had no responsibilities here?" The High King spoke slowly, without looking at Corum.

"I think so. Ilbrec is for the venture."

"Your chances of survival would seem to be exceptionally slender."

"Perhaps." Corum rubbed at his eye-patch. "But then if we cared considerably about our survival we would not be engaged in this war against the Fhoi Myore."

"That is reasonable," said Amergin.

Corum tried to interpret the import of what Amergin was saying. "There are many reasons," he said, "why I should lead the Mabden. Morale must be kept as high as possible while we march through the cold lands."

"True," said Amergin. "I have been debating all this

in my mind, as no doubt have you. But you will remember that I asked you earlier to persuade Goffanon to reveal the nature of these potential allies?"

"You spoke of it this morning."

"Exactly. Well, since then I have meditated on this whole matter further and my conclusions are the same—we shall fare badly at Caer Llud. We shall be defeated by the Fhoi Myore unless we have magical assistance. We require supernatural aid, Prince Corum, beyond anything I can summon, beyond anything the Sidhi have at their disposal. And it appears that the only place from whence such help can be got is Ynys Scaith. I tell you all this knowing that you are discreet. Needless to say, our armies must set forth with every confidence of defeating the Fhoi Myore. Their morale would be harmed if you did not lead them, yet I think even with your leadership we should still be beaten. Thus, reluctantly, I conclude that our only hope lies in your being able to bargain with the folk of Ynys Scaith to come to our assistance."

"And what if I fail?"

"Dying men will curse you for a traitor, but your name will not be dishonored for long, for there will be no Mabden left to hate you."

"Is there no other way. What of the lost treasures of the Mabden, the Sidhi gifts?"

"Those that remain are in Fhoi Myore hands. The Healing Cauldron is at Caer Llud. So is the Collar of Power. There was one other, but we were never sure of its nature or why it was amongst our treasures. That is lost."

"What was it?"

"An old saddle of cracked leather. We kept it faithfully, as we kept our other treasures, but I think it came with them by mistake."

"So you cannot recover this cauldron and collar until the Fhoi Myore are defeated."

"Just so."

"Do you know anything more of the folk of Ynys Scaith?"

"Only that they would, if they could, leave this plane of ours forever."

"So I have learned. Yet we are not, surely, powerful enough to help them to do this."

"If I had the Collar of Power," said Amergin, "I might, with other knowledge, be able to achieve their end for them."

"Goffanon thinks that any bargain with the folk of the Shadow Isle will cost us dear—too dear."

"If some of us survive, the cost will not be too much," said Amergin, "and I think some of us would live on."

"Perhaps life is not at stake. What other damage could they do?"

"I do not know. If you think the risk too great . . ."

"I have my own reasons, as well as yours, for visiting Ynys Scaith," Corum said.

"It would be best if you left without much ceremony," Amergin told him. "I would inform our men that you have embarked upon a quest and that you will, if possible, rejoin us before the attack on Caer Llud. In the meantime, if Goffanon will not go to Ynys Scaith, let us hope he will lead the Mabden in your stead, for he knows Caer Llud."

"But he has a weakness, remember that," said Corum. "The wizard Calatin has power over him which can only be broken if Calatin loses the bag of spittle he holds. When you attack Caer Llud and if I have perished, seek Calatin out and slay him at once. I think of all those who side with the Fhoi Myore that Calatin is the most dangerous, for he is the most human."

"I will remember what you say," answered the Archdruid. "But I do not think you will perish upon Ynys Scaith, Corum."

"Perhaps not." Corum frowned. "Yet I sense that this world becomes increasingly inhospitable to me, as it does to the folk of the Isle of Shadows."

"You could speak truly," Amergin agreed. "The specific conjunction of the planes might, in your case, be unlucky."

Corum smiled. "That sounds like mysticism of doubtful veracity, High King."

"Truth often sounds so." The Archdruid rose. "When would you set forth for Ynys Scaith?"

"Soon. I must consult Ilbrec."

"Leave all other things to me," said Amergin, "and, I beg you, do not discuss our plan too fully with anyone, even Medhbh."

"Very well." Corum watched Amergin leave, wondering if the Archdruid were playing an even more complex game than he had guessed and that Corum was a piece he was preparing to sacrifice. He shrugged the thoughts away. Amergin's logic was good, particularly if his vision had been accurate and the Mabden army stood the chance of being totally defeated at Caer Llud. And soon after Amergin had gone, Corum followed him, making his way out of the fortress city, down the hill to Ilbrec's great tent.

Corum had returned to his chambers and was arming himself when Medhbh came in. She had expected to find him asleep and instead saw him dressed for war. "What's this? Do we march tomorrow?"

Corum shook his head. "I go to Ynys Scaith," he told her.

"You embark upon a private quest when you are due to lead us against Caer Llud?" She laughed, wishing to believe that he joked.

Corum remembered Amergin's wish that he should say as little as possible about his reasons for the journey. "It is not a private quest," he replied. "Not wholly, at any rate."

"No?" Her voice was shaking. She paced the room several times before continuing. "We should never have trusted one not of our own race. Why should we expect you to feel loyalty to our cause?"

"You know that I feel that loyalty, Medhbh." He walked toward her, arms outstretched, but she shook his hand away, turning to glare at him.

"You go to madness and death if you go to Ynys Scaith. You heard what Artek told us!" She tried to control her emotion. "If you go to Caer Llud with us, the worst that can happen to you is that your death will be a noble one."

"I will rejoin you at Caer Llud if that is possible. The army will travel much slower than shall I. There is every chance of my rejoining it even before the assault on Caer Llud."

"There is every chance of your never returning from Ynys Scaith," she said grimly.

He shrugged.

This gesture angered her further. Some word came half-formed from her lips, then she had walked to the door opened it and shut it with a crash behind her.

Corum began to follow her, then thought better of it, knowing that further argument would lead to further misunderstanding. He hoped that Amergin might explain his predicament to Medhbh at some time, or at least convince her that his need to visit Ynys Scaith was not wholly the result of a private obsession.

But it was with a heavy heart indeed that he left the castle and returned to the camp where Ilbrec awaited him.

The golden giant was caparisoned for war, his great sword Retaliator sheathed at his hip, his huge horse Splendid Mane prepared for riding. He was smiling, plainly excited by the prospect of their adventure; but Corum could feel nothing but pain as he tried to return the Sidhi's smile.

"There is no time to waste," said Ilbrec. "As we agreed, we shall both ride Splendid Mane. He gallops faster than any mortal horse and will have us to Ynys Scaith and back in no time. I got the chart from Kawanh. There is naught else to keep us here."

"No," said Corum. "Naught else."

"You are irresponsible fools!"

Corum wheeled round to confront a Goffanon whose face was dark with rage. The Sidhi dwarf shook the fist which held his double-bladed war-axe and he snarled at them. "If you come back from Ynys Scaith alive then you will not be sane. You will be good for nothing. We need you on this march. The Mabden are expecting the three of us to lead them. Our presence gives them confidence. Do not go to Ynys Scaith. Do not go!"

"Goffanon," said Ilbrec reasonably, "in most things I respect your wisdom. In this matter, however, we must follow our own instincts."

"Your instincts are false if they lead you to destruction, to the betrayal of those you have sworn to serve! Do not go!"

"We go," said Corum in a quiet voice. "We must."

"Then an evil demon drives you an! you are no longer my friends," said Goffanon. "You are no longer my friends."

"You should respect our motives, Goffanon . . ." began Corum, but he was cut off by the dwarf's cursing.

"Even if you return sane from Ynys Scaith—and I doubt that you will—you will bring your own doom with you. That is unquestionable. I have seen it. There has been a hint of it in my dreams of late."

With a certain defiance, Corum said: "The Vadhagh had a theory that dreams tell more about the man who dreams than about the world he dwells in. Could you have other motives for not wishing us to visit Ynys Scaith . . . ?"

Goffanon glared at him contemptuously. "I go with the Mabden to Caer Llud," he said.

"Be careful of Calatin," said Corum earnestly.

"I think that Calatin was a better friend than are you two." Goffanon's back was bowed as he made to leave the camp.

"Well, must I decide?" The voice was light and ironic. It belonged to Jhary-a-Conel, who had emerged from the shadows and stood with his hand on his hip, his other hand to his chin, staring at the three of them from under tightly-drawn brows. "Must I decide between traveling to Ynys Scaith or Caer Llud? Are my loyalties divided?"

"You go to Caer Llud," said Corum. "Your wisdom and knowledge are required here. They are greater than mine . . ."

"Whose would not be?" burst out Goffanon, still with his back to Corum.

"Go with Goffanon, Jhary," said Corum softly to the Companion to Champions. "Help guard him against Calatin's sorcerery."

Jhary nodded. He touched Corum on the shoulder. "Goodbye, treacherous friend," he murmured. And the little smile on his lips was melancholy.

As they spoke, Ilbrec mounted Splendid Mane, his harness clattering. "Corum?"

Corum spoke sharply. "Goffanon. I am sure that I do what is most necessary to serve our cause best."

"You will pay a price," said Goffanon. "You will pay, Corum. Heed my warning."

Corum tapped a silver finger against the sword he now wore at his side. "My danger is lessened, however, thanks to your gift. I have faith in this blade you made. Do you say it will not protect me at all?"

Shaking his huge head from side to side as if in pain, Goffanon groaned. "That depends upon the uses to which it is put. But, by the souls of all the Sidhi heroes, great and dead, I wish that I had not forged it."

BOOK TWO

On Ynys Scaith many terrors are experienced, many deceptions revealed, and several reversals brought about.

THE ENCHANTMENTS OF YNYS SCAITH

Splendid Mane had not forgotten the old roads between the planes and now the Sidhi horse galloped apparently upon the very waters of the sea as dawn found Ilbrec and Corum, both mounted on the same steed, out of sight of any land at all. The cool ocean rolled, blue, veined with white, on all sides of them, turning to pink, to gold and back to blue again as the sun climbed the sky.

"Amergin said that Shadow Isle existed even before the coming of the Sidhi." Corum sat behind Ilbrec, clinging to the giant's great belt. "Yet you told me it only came to this plane when the Sidhi came."

"There were always adepts in certain arts who could travel between the planes, as you well know," explained Ilbrec, delighting in the feel of the spray upon his face, "and doubtless there were Mabden druids who visited Ynys Scaith before it properly arrived here."

"And who, originally, were the folk who dwell now upon Ynys Scaith? Were they Mabden?"

"Never. An older race, like the Vadhagh, who were gradually superceded by Mabden. Living in virtual exile upon their island they became inbred and cruel—and they had already been inbred and cruel before the island became their only home."

"And what was this race called?"

"That I do not know." Ilbrec drew Kawanh's chart from inside his armor, inspecting the parchment closely and then leaning forward to murmur something in the ear of Splendid Mane.

Almost at once the horse began to alter its direction slightly, making for the northwest.

Gray clouds began to appear, bringing with them a light rain which was not particularly uncomfortable, and soon they had passed into the sunshine again. Corum found himself half-asleep as he clung to Ilbrec's belt, and he deliberately took the opportunity to rest his body and his mind as much as possible, knowing that he would need all his resources when they came to Ynys Scaith.

And now it was that the two heroes rode across the sea and came at length to Ynys Scaith: a small island, shaped like the peak of a mountain and shrouded by dark cloud where all about it the sky was blue and clear. They could hear the breakers booming on its bleak beaches, they could see the hill at the island's very center, and soon they saw the single tall pine standing upon the top of the hill; but of the rest of the island, though they rode still closer, they could make out little. With a soft word and a light movement of his hand Ilbrec reined in Splendid Mane, and the horse and its riders came to a halt while the sea swirled everywhere around them.

Corum adjusted his silvered, conical helm upon his head and leaned to tighten the straps of his greaves of gilded brass, at the same time shrugging his silver byrnie into a more comfortable fit upon his body. Over his shoulder went his quiver of arrows and his unstrung bow. Onto his left arm went his shield of white hide, and now he clenched a long-hafted war-axe in his silver hand, leaving his right hand free to clutch Ilbrec's belt or to draw his strange sword when the occasion demanded. In front of him Ilbrec threw back his heavy cloak so that the sun glanced off his golden, braided hair, his bronze armor and shield, and his bracelets of gold. He turned to look back at Corum, and his green-grey eyes were identical in color to the sea. And Ilbrec smiled. "Are you ready, friend Corum?"

Corum could not imitate the devil-may-care smile of the Sidhi; his own smile was a little grimmer as he inclined his head slightly. "Let us ride on to Ynys Scaith," he said.

So Ilbrec shook Splendid Mane's reins and the huge

81

horse began to gallop again, the spray rising high into the air as they went faster and faster toward the isle of enchantments.

Now Splendid Mane was almost upon the beach, yet it was still impossible to define any clear images in the general, shadowy appearance of the island. There was a suggestion of heavy, tangled forest, of half-ruined buildings, of beaches littered with a variety of flotsam, of swirling mist, of large-winged flapping birds, of burly beasts prowling through the wreckage and the trees, but every time the eye seemed about to focus on something it would shift again and become dim. Once Corum thought he saw a great face, larger than Ilbrec's, staring at him from over a rock, but then both face and rock seemed to become a tree, or a building, or a beast. There was something unclean and dolorous about Ynys Scaith; it had none of the beauty of Hy-Breasail. It was almost as if this particular magic isle were the reverse of the first Corum had visited. Soft, unpleasant sounds issued from the interior; sometimes it was as if voices whispered to him. A smell of corruption was carried to his nostrils by an unpleasant wind. Ynys Scaith's chief impression was one of decay—of a soul in decay—and in this it had something in common with the Fhoi Myore. Corum was filled with foreboding. Why should the folk of Ynys Scaith throw in their lot with the Mabden? They would seem likelier to wish to help the Cold Folk.

Again Ilbrec reined in Splendid Mane, a foot or two from the shore, and he flung up his left hand, calling out:

"Hail, Ynys Scaith! We are willing visitors to your land! Would you welcome us?"

It was an old greeting, a traditional Mabden greeting, but Corum felt it would mean little to whomever dwelled in this place.

"Hail, Ynys Scaith! We come in peace to discuss a bargain with you!" called the gigantic youth.

There was a suggestion of an echo, but no other reply. Ilbrec shrugged. "Then we must visit the island uninvited. Poor courtesy . . ."

"Which could well be returned by the inhabitants," said Corum.

Ilbrec urged Splendid Mane forward and the horse's hooves at last touched the gray beach of Ynys Scaith, whereupon the forest ahead of them turned suddenly to blazing scarlet fronds, agitated and whimpering, rustling and chuckling. Looking back, Corum could no longer see the sea. Instead he saw a wall of liquid lead.

Deliberately, Ilbrec rode toward the fronds and, as he approached, they flattened themselves like suppliants hailing a conqueror. Splendid Mane, disturbed and unwilling to continue, snorted and set his ears back, but Ilbrec clapped his heels against the beast's flanks and on they went. No sooner had they crossed a few feet of these fronds than they sprang up again and the two heroes were surrounded by the plants which reached feathery fingers out and touched their flesh and sighed.

And Corum felt that the fronds reached through his skin and stroked his bones and he was hard put not to lash out at the things with his sword. He could understand the terror of the Mabden when confronted with such monstrous foliage, but he had experienced much more in his time and knew how to control his panic. He attempted to speak casually to Ilbrec, who also pretended to ignore the plants.

"Interesting flora, Ilbrec. I've seen nothing like it elsewhere upon this plane."

"Indeed it is, friend Corum." Ilbrec's voice shook only a little. "It seems to have some kind of primitive intelligence."

The whispering increased, the touch of the plants became more insistent, but the two rode steadfastly on through the forest, their eyes aching from the scarlet blaze.

"Could this be an illusion, even?" Corum suggested.

"Possibly, my friend. A clever one."

The fronds thinned, giving way to pavements of green marble which lay beneath an inch or two of yellowish liquid smelling several times worse than a stagnant pond. All kinds of small insect life existed in the liquid and occasionally clouds of flying things would rise out of it and hover around their heads as if inspecting them. To their right were several ruins: colonnades covered in festering ivy, partially collapsed galleries, walls of rotting granite and eroded quartz on which grew vines whose livid blooms emitted a sickly stench; while ahead of them they could see two-legged animals bending to drink the liquid, looking at them through glazed, white eyes before stooping to drink again. Something wriggled across Splendid Mane's path. Corum thought at first he had seen a pale snake, but then he wondered if the thing had not had the shape of a human being. He looked for it, but it had disappeared. An ordinary black rat swam steadily through the deeper reaches of the liquid; it ignored Ilbrec and Corum. Then it dived and disappeared through a narrow crack in the surface of the marble.

By the time they had reached the far side of this expanse the two-legged creatures had gone and Splendid Mane walked on a lawn of spongy grass which gave off disgusting sucking noises whenever the horse pulled its hooves free. So far nothing had menaced them directly and Corum began to think that the Mabden who had landed here had been victims of their own terrors instilled in them by such ghastly sights as these. Now his nose detected a stench not unlike that of cow dung, but rather stronger. It was a nauseating stench and he drew a scarf from under his byrnie and tied it around his mouth, though it made only the slightest difference. Ilbrec cleared his throat and spat upon the turf, guiding Splendid Mane toward a pathway of cracked lapis lazuli leading into a dark corridor of trees which were like and yet unlike ordinary rhododendrons. Large, dark, sticky leaves brushed their faces and soon the corridor had become pitch black, save for a few yellow lights which flickered in the recesses of the foliage on both sides of them. Once or twice it seemed to Corum that the lights revealed grinning faces whose features had been partially eaten away, but he guessed that his imagination, fed by the obscene visions of the recent past, was responsible for these sights.

"Let us hope this path leads us somewhere," murmured Ilbrec. "The stench gets worse, if anything. Could it be, I wonder, the distinctive odor of Ynys Scaith's inhabitants?"

"Let us hope not, Ilbrec. It will make communication with them that much more difficult. Do you know in what direction we head now?"

"I fear not," replied the Sidhi youth. "I am not sure if we go south, north, east, or west. All I know is that the branches above us are getting damnedably low and it would be wise if I, at least, dismounted. Will you take a grip on the saddle, Corum, while I get off?"

Corum did so and felt Ilbrec get down from his saddle, heard the creak of harness and a jingle as Ilbrec took Splendid Mane's reins and began to plod on. Without the bulk of the giant to reassure him, Corum felt much more exposed to the dangers—imaginary or otherwise—of this reeking arbor. Did he hear laughter from the depths on either side? Did he hear bodies moving menacingly, keeping pace with him, ready to pounce? Was that a hand which reached out and pinched his leg?

More lights flickered, but this time they were directly ahead.

Something coughed in the forest.

Corum took a firmer grip on his sword. "Do you feel we are watched, Ilbrec?"

"It is possible." The young giant's voice was firm, but tense.

"Everything we have seen speaks of a great civilization which died a thousand years ago. Perhaps there are no longer any intelligent inhabitants on Ynys Scaith?"

"Perhaps . . ."

"Perhaps we have only animals to fear—and diseases. Could the air affect the brain and infest it with unpleasant thoughts, terrifying visions?"

"Who knows?"

And the voice which replied to Corum was not Ilbrec's voice.

"Ilbrec?" whispered Corum, afraid that his friend had suddenly vanished.

There was a pause.

"Ilbrec?"

"I heard it also," said Ilbrec and Corum heard him move back a pace and reach out a huge hand to touch Corum's arm and squeeze it gently. Then Ilbrec raised his voice: "Where are you? Who was it that spoke to us?"

But there came no further reply and so they pressed on, coming at length to a place where thin sunlight broke through the branches and the tunnel divided into three separate paths. The shortest was the middle one for, though it was gloomy, the sky could be seen at its far end.

"This would seem the best," Ilbrec said, remounting. "What think you, Corum?"

Corum shrugged. "It is tempting—almost a trap," he said. "As if the folk of Ynys Scaith wished to lure us somewhere."

Ilbrec said: "Let them lure us, if they will."

"My feelings, too."

Without further comment, Ilbrec urged Splendid Mane into the tunnel.

Slowly the lattice above them opened out until the cracked path widened and they rode down an avenue of stunted bushes, seeing ahead of them tall, broken columns around which climbed the stems of some long-dead lichen, brown and black and dark green. And it was only when they had passed between those columns, carved with demonic creatures and grinning, bestial heads, that they realized they were now upon a bridge built over an immensely wide and dreadfully deep chasm. Once there had been a wall on either side of the bridge, but in most places the wall had fallen away and they could see down to the floor of the chasm, where a stretch of black water boiled and in which reptilian bodies of all descriptions threshed and snapped and yelled.

And over the bridge there now moaned a miserable wind, a cold, clinging wind which dragged at their cloaks and even seemed to threaten to toss them off the swaying stonework of the bridge and down into the chasm.

Ilbrec sniffed, tugging his cloak about him, looking over the edge with an expression of distaste upon his features.

"They are large, those reptiles. I have seen none larger. Look at the teeth they have in their mouths! Look at those glaring eyes, those boney crests, those horns. Ach! I am glad they cannot reach us, Corum!"

And Corum nodded his agreement.

"This is no world for a Sidhi," Ilbrec murmured.

"Nor a Vadhagh," said Corum.

By the time they had reached the middle of the bridge the wind had increased and Splendid Mane found it difficult to push even his great bulk against it. It was then that Corum looked up and saw what he thought at first were birds. There were about a score of them, flying in a rough formation, and as they came closer he saw that they were not birds at all but winged reptiles with long snouts filled with sharp, yellow fangs. He tapped Ilbrec upon his shoulder, pointing.

"Ilbrec," he said. "Dragons."

They were dragons, indeed, albeit scarcely larger than the great eagles which inhabited the northern mountains of Bro-an-Mabden, and they were plainly bent on attacking the two who sat upon Splendid Mane's back.

Corum stuck his feet into the horse's girth strap so that the wind should not blow him from its back and with some difficulty managed to unsling his bow, string it, and take an arrow from his quiver. He fitted the arrow to the string, drew it back, sighted along the arrow, did his best to allow for the strength of the wind, and let fly at the nearest dragon. His arrow missed the beast's body, but pierced the wing. The dragon yelled, twisted in the air, snapping at the arrow with its teeth. It began to fall, righted itself clumsily, but then began to spin round and round, falling toward the dark water below where other reptiles hungrily awaited it. Two more arrows Corum let fly, but both went wide of their targets. Then a dragon swept in at Ilbrec's head and its teeth grazed against the rim of the giant's shield as he put it up to defend himself, at the same time swinging Retaliator up in an attempt to stab the dragon's belly. Splendid Mane reared, whinnying, hooves flailing, eyes rolling, and the bridge shuddered at this new movement. A fresh crack appeared in it and a piece at the edge broke off and tumbled into the gorge. Corum felt his stomach turn as he saw the masonry go hurtling down. He shot another arrow and this again missed its mark completely, but plunged into the throat of the next dragon. But now they were surrounded by the flap of leathery wings, the snap of sharp teeth, and claws almost like human hands reached out to tear at them. Corum had to drop the bow and draw his unnamed sword, Goffanon's gift. Half-blinded by the silvery light which issued from the metal, he slashed at random at the attacking reptiles and felt the beautifully honed blade slice into cold-blooded flesh. Now wounded dragons scuttled around Splendid Mane's legs and, from the corner of his eye, Corum saw at least three fall over the jagged edge of the bridge. And Corum saw Ilbrec's bright, golden sword all dripping with the dragons' blood and he heard the voice of the youth as he sang a Sidhi song (for it was ever the Sidhi way to sing when death confronted them).

> Foes from the east we ever faced;
> And fearless foes they were.
> In fifty fights the Sidhi fought,
> Ere they were clad in gore.
> Fierce were we in war.
> Fierce were we in war.

Corum felt something settle on his back and cold claws touched his flesh. With a shout he slashed backwards and his blade carved into scaley skin and brittle bone and a dragon coughed and vomited blood over his silvered helm. Clearing the chill and sticky stuff from his eye, Corum was in time to stab upward at a dragon who dived down at Ilbrec's unprotected head, its claws outstretched.

And Ilbrec sang on:

Lest Sidhi bodies clay should claim,
Pray let that clay be known.
Let moral heroes sing our fame,
In Sidhi soil rest Sidhi bones.
In foreign earth we lie alone.
In foreign earth we lie alone.

Corum guessed the meaning of Ilbrec's song, for he,
too, disliked the idea of his life being stolen by these
mindless creatures, of dying in this nameless place with
none knowing how he died.

At least half the dragons had now been slain or so
badly wounded that they were harmless, but the
movement of the great Sidhi steed as he reared and tram-
pled the corpses of the reptiles was causing more and
more pieces of masonry to fall from the bridge and now
a sizeable hole had appeared ahead of them. His attention divided between the potential disaster and the immediate one, Corum failed to see a dragon swoop in on
him, its claws digging into his shoulders, its snout snapping at his face. With a strangled gasp he brought his
shield rim up, jamming it into the dragon's soft belly
and at the same time forcing his unnamed sword into the
thing's throat. The reptile's corpse lost its grip and
flopped onto the stone of the bridge and at that moment
the bridge itself gave way and Ilbrec, Splendid Mane and
Corum were hurtling downward to where the swimming
things swarmed in the black waters of the chasm.

Corum heard Ilbrec yelling:

"Cling to my belt, Corum. At all costs do not lose your
grip."

And though Corum obeyed, he saw little point in the
Sidhi's instructions. After all, they were soon to be dead.
But first, of course, would come the pain. He hoped it
would not last too long.

The Second Chapter

THE MELIBANN REVEAL THEMSELVES

There was a moment when they were falling and then a moment when they were rising, but Corum, preparing himself for death, had not noticed when the change had come about. Somewhat circuitously, Splendid Mane appeared to be galloping into the sky, back toward the broken bridge. The dragons had gone, doubtless unwilling to follow their quarry down to the bottom of the chasm and contest ownership with their larger cousins.

And Ilbrec was laughing, guessing what Corum must feel.

"The old roads are everywhere," he said, "and thank my ancestors that Splendid Mane can still find them!"

The horse slowed to a leisurely trot, still apparently treading thin air, and then continued toward the far edge of the chasm.

Corum sighed with relief. For all that he had good reason to trust Splendid Mane's powers, it was hard for him to believe in the horse's ability to ride across the water, let alone the air. Once again the hooves touched ground which Corum could see was solid, and the horse came to a halt. Another pathway led through low hills covered in a kind of fungus, multicolored, unhealthy. Ilbrec and Corum dismounted to inspect their wounds. Corum had lost his bow and his quiver was empty—he threw it aside—but the dragons' claws had produced little more than flesh wounds in his arms and shoulders. Ilbrec was similarly unharmed. They grinned at each other and it was plain to both that neither had expected to live on that shuddering bridge.

Ilbrec took his water bottle from his saddle bag and offered it to Corum. It was the size of a small barrel and Corum had difficulty lifting it to his lips, but he was grateful for the drink.

"What puzzles me," said Ilbrec, accepting the bottle

back and raising it, "is the size of Ynys Scaith. From the sea it looks a comparatively small island. Yet from here it appears to be a sizeable land, going on as far as the eye can see. And look—" he pointed into the distance where the hill and the single pine tree stood out sharply, though the scenery all around it was misty—"the hill seems further away from us than ever. There is no question in my mind, Corum, that this place is under a glamor of considerable power."

"Aye," agreed the Vadhagh Prince, "and I have the feeling that we have hardly begun to understand the extent of it as yet."

With this, they remounted and followed the path on through the hills until they turned a corner and saw that the hills ended sharply, giving way to a plain seemingly made of hammered copper, shimmering as it reflected the light of the sun, and far away, in what Corum judged to be the center of this plain, some figures stood. Whether the figures were of beasts or of men, Corum could not tell, but he loosened Goffanon's gift-sword in its sheath and he adjusted the shield more firmly upon his arm as Splendid Mane began to trot over the plain, his hooves ringing and clanging as they struck the metal.

Corum put his hand to his eyes to protect them against the glare of the copper, straining to make out more detail, but it was a long time before he was certain that the figures were indeed human and a longer time before he realized that they were Mabden—men, women and children—and that only a few of the group stood upright. Most lay upon the plain of hammered copper and were very still.

Ilbrec shook Splendid Mane's reins and the great horse slowed to a walk.

"Artek's people?" said Ilbrec.

"It would seem so," said Corum. "They have a similar look to them."

Still a little wary, the two dismounted again and began to walk toward the group of figures who now stood in such sharp outline against the landscape of hammered copper.

As they came within earshot they began to hear voices —small moans, whimperings, groans and whispers—and they saw that all were naked and that most of those upon the ground were dead. All appeared to have been burned by fire. Those who stood had red, blistered skins and it was a wonder that they could remain upon their feet at all. Corum could feel the heat of the hammered copper through his thick-soled boots and he could imagine how fierce it must be on bare feet. These people could not have come willingly unclad to the center of the plain; they had been driven here. They were dying, roasting to death. Some cruel intelligence had forced them here. Corum swallowed his anger, finding it almost impossible to understand the minds of creatures who could conceive of such a cruelty. He noticed now that several of the men and women had their hands tied behind them and that they were trying, futilely, to protect those few children who still remained alive.

As they realized that Corum and Ilbrec had come, the Mabden peered at them in fear through parblind eyes. Blistered lips moved pleadingly.

"We are not your enemies," said Corum. "We are friends of Artek. Are you the People of Fyean?"

One man turned his ruined face toward Corum. His voice was like the sound of a distant wind. "We are. All that remain."

"Who did this to you?"

"The island. Ynys Scaith."

"How did you come to the plain?"

"Have you not seen the centaurs—and the monstrous spiders?"

Corum shook his head. "We came over the bridge. Over the chasm where the giant reptiles dwell."

"There is no chasm . . ."

Corum paused, then said: "There was for us."

Drawing a small knife from his belt he stepped forward to untie the man's hands, but the wretch stumbled backward fearfully.

"We are friends," Corum told him again. "We have

92

spoken with Artek who told us what had befallen you. It is largely because we met him that we came here."

"Artek is safe?" A woman spoke. It was possible that she was young, that she had been beautiful. "He is safe?" She stumbled toward Corum. Her hands, also, were secured behind her back. She fell and struggled to her knees, whimpering in pain. "Artek?"

"He is safe—and about a score more of your folk."

"Ah," she breathed. "Oh, I am glad . . ."

"His wife," said the man to whom Corum had first spoken. But Corum had already guessed this. "Did Artek send you here to rescue her?"

"To rescue you all," said Corum. It was a lie he was happy to tell. These people were dying. It would not be long before the last perished.

"Then you are too late," said Artek's wife.

Corum stopped to cut her bonds, and then the voice he had heard in the forest came again from nowhere:

"Do not free her. She is ours now."

Corum looked about him but, save that the air seemed to shimmer all the more, he could see nothing.

"I shall free her, however," he said. "So that she might at least die with her hands unbound."

"Why do you seek to anger us?"

"I seek to anger no one. I am Corum Llaw Ereint." He held up his silver hand. "I am the Champion Eternal. I came in peace to Ynys Scaith. I mean no harm to its inhabitants—but I will not see further harm done to these people."

"Corum . . ." began Ilbrec softly, his hand upon the hilt of Retaliator. "I think we confront, at last, the folk of Ynys Scaith."

Corum ignored him and cut the ropes away from the woman's burned flesh.

"Corum . . ."

Methodically Corum went amongst the folk of Fyean and he offered them his water bottle and those who were bound he untied. He looked nowhere else.

"Corum!"

Ilbrec's voice was more urgent and when Corum had

finished his work and looked up he saw that Ilbrec and Splendid Mane were surrounded by tall, slim figures of a brownish yellow color, whose skins were seamed and whose hair was sparse.

They wore little more than belts supporting large swords. The flesh of their lips was drawn back from their teeth, their cheeks were sunken, as were their eyes, and they had the appearance of corpses long preserved. When they moved, small pieces of dried skin or flesh fell from their bodies. If they had expressions upon their faces, Corum could not tell what they were. He could only stand and look upon them in horror.

One wore a spiked crown set with sapphires and rubies. The precious stones seemed to contain more life than did his face and body. White eyes peered at Corum; yellow teeth clashed as the being spoke.

"We are the Malibann and this island is our home. We have a right to protect ourselves against invaders." His accent was unusual but his words were easy to understand. "We are ancient . . ."

Ilbrec nodded a sardonic agreement. The Malibann leader was quick to notice Ilbrec's expression. He inclined his mummified head. "We use these bodies rarely," he said by way of explanation. "But be assured that we have little need of them. It is not in physical prowess that we pride ourselves, but in our wizardly power."

"It is great," agreed Ilbrec.

"We are ancient," continued the leader, "and we know much. We can control almost anything we wish to control. We can stop the sun from rising, should we wish it."

"Then why exact petty spite upon these people?" Corum asked him. "These are not the actions of demigods!"

"It is our whim to punish those who invaded our island."

"They meant you no harm. They were forced upon your shores by unkind elements."

Studying the horrible, decaying faces of the Malibann,

Corum became slowly aware that in many ways they shared characteristics of features with the Vadhagh. He wondered if these were Vadhagh folk, exiled centuries before. Were they the original inhabitants of Ynys Scaith?

"How they came—how you came—is immaterial to us. You came—they came—you must be punished."

"Are all who land here punished?" Ilbrec asked thoughtfully.

"Almost all," said the leader of the Malibann. "It depends upon their reasons for visiting us."

"We came to speak with you," said Corum. "We came to offer help in return for aid from you."

"What can you offer the Malibann?"

"Escape," said Corum, "from this plane—back to a plane more hospitable to you."

"That matter is already in hand."

Corum was astonished. "You have help?"

"The Malibann never seek help. We have employed someone to perform a service for us."

"Someone of this world?"

"Yes. But now we grow weary of conversing with such primitive intellects as yourselves. First we shall dismiss this filth."

The eyes of the Malibann glowed a fiery red. There came a shrill, despairing wailing from the people of Fyean and then they had all vanished. And with them vanished the plain of hammered copper. Now Corum and Ilbrec and Splendid Mane stood in a hall whose roof had partially fallen in. Evening sunshine filtered through the gaps in roof and walls and revealed rotting tapestries, crumbling sculpture, faded murals.

"Where is this place?" Corum asked of the Malibann who stood in the shadows near the walls.

The leader laughed. "You do not recognize it? Why, it is where all your adventures took place—or most of them."

"What? Within the confines of this hall?" Ilbrec stared around him in dismay. "But how could such a thing have been accomplished?"

"We have great powers, the Malibann, and I, Sactric, have the greatest power of all, that is why I am Emperor of Malibann . . ."

"This isle? You style it an empire?" Ilbrec smiled faintly.

"This isle is the hub of an empire so magnificent it would make your most marvellous civilization seem like the encampment of a baboon tribe. When we return to our own plane—from which we were banished by a trick—we shall reclaim that empire and Sactric shall reign over it."

"Who is it that aids you in this ambition?" Corum asked. "One of the Fhoi Myore?"

"The Fhoi Myore? The Fhoi Myore are merely mad beasts. What help could they give us? No, we have a subtler ally. We await his return at this moment. Perhaps we shall let you live long enough to meet him."

Ilbrec murmured to Corum. "The sun is only just setting. Can we have been here such a short time?"

And Sactric laughed at him. "Is two months a short time in your terms?"

"Two months? What mean you?" Corum made a movement toward Sactric.

"I mean only that the passage of time on Ynys Scaith and the passage of time in your world proceed at different speeds. Effectively, Corum Llaw Ereint, you have been here for at least two months."

A SHIP COMES SAILING TO THE ISLE OF SHADOWS

"Ah, Ilbrec," said Corum to his friend, "then how have the Mabden fared against the Fhoi Myore?"

Ilbrec could not reply to this. Instead he shook his head, saying: "Goffanon spoke the truth. We were fools. We should not have come here."

"At least we are all agreed in one thing," came Sactric's dry voice from the shadows. The gems in his crown glinted as he moved. "And having heard that admission I am inclined to spare your lives for a while. Moreover I shall grant you the freedom of this island you call Ynys Scaith." Then, rather more casually than would seem necessary to him, he added, "You know one named Goffanon?"

"We do," said Ilbrec. "He warned us against coming here."

"Goffanon is sensible, it seems."

"Aye. It seems so," said Corum. He was still angry, still bewildered, still considering attacking Sactric, though he guessed he would have little satisfaction even if he managed to put to the sword that already dead body. "You are acquainted with him?"

"He visited us once. Now we must deal with your horse." Sactric's eyes began to glow red as he gestured toward Splendid Mane. Ilbrec cried out and ran to his steed but already Splendid Mane's pupils became fixed and glazed and the horse was frozen to the spot.

"He is not harmed," said Sactric. "He is too valuable for that. When you are dead, we shall use him."

"If he will let you," muttered Ilbrec ferociously, into his beard.

Then the Malibann withdrew into the deeper shadows and were gone.

Listlessly the two heroes climbed through the ruins

and out into what remained of the evening light. Now they saw the island for what it really was. Save for the hill (at whose foot they now stood) and the single pine, the rest of the island was a wasteland of flotsam, of carrion, of decaying stone, vegetation, metal, and bones. Here were the remains of all the ships which had ever landed on the shores of Ynys Scaith, and here were the remains, too, of their cargoes and their crews. Rusting armor and weapons lay all about; yellow bones of men and of their beasts were much in evidence, some complete skeletons, some scattered, while occasionally Corum and Ilbrec came upon a pile consisting entirely of skulls or another pile consisting of rib-cages. Weatherrotted fabrics, silks, woolens, cotton garments, fluttered in the chill wind which also bore a faint, terrible stink of putrefaction; leather breastplates, jerkins, caps, horse furniture, boots and gauntlets, were cracked, disintegrating. Iron and bronze and brass weapons lay rusted together in heaps, jewels had lost their sheen and looked sickly, as if they, too, rotted; gray ash blew like an evermoving tide across these scenes and nowhere was there any evidence of a living creature, not even a raven or a cur to feast upon those bodies still fresh enough to have flesh on their bones.

"In a way I prefer the Malibann illusions," said Ilbrec, "for all that they were terrifying and came close to killing us!"

"The reality is in a sense more terrifying," murmured Corum, pulling his cloak about him as he stumbled over the waste of detritus, following Ilbrec. The night was closing in and Corum did not look forward to spending it surrounded by so much evidence of death.

Ilbrec's eye had been casting through the gloom as the giant had walked, and now it fixed on something. Ilbrec paused, changed his direction a little, and plunged through rubble until he came to an overturned chariot which still had the bones of a horse between its shafts. He reached into the chariot and the skeleton of the driver fell with a clatter at the movement. Ignoring this,

Ilbrec straightened his back, holding something dusty and shapeless in his hand. He frowned.

"What have you found, Ilbrec?" Corum asked, reaching his companion's side.

"I am not sure, Vadhagh friend."

Corum inspected Ilbrec's discovery. It was an old saddle of cracked leather; its straps did not seem strong enough to hold it to the lightest of horses. The buckles were dull, rusty and half falling off, and altogether Corum considered it the most worthless of discoveries.

"An old saddle . . ."

"Just so."

"Splendid Mane has a good saddle of his own. Besides, that would not fit him. It is made for a mortal horse."

Ilbrec nodded. "As you say, it would not fit him." But he held onto the saddle as they made their way down to the beach and found a place relatively clear of debris, settling down to rest, since there was little else to do that night.

But before he went to sleep, Ilbrec sat cross-legged, turning the old saddle over and over in his great hands. And once Corum heard him murmur:

"Are we all that are left, we two? Are we the last?"

And then the morning dawned.

First the water was white and wide and then it turned slowly to scarlet, as if some great dying sea-beast beneath the surface were spreading its life-blood in its final throes, and it pulsed as the red sun rose, making the sky blossom with deep yellows and watery purples and a flat, rich orange.

And the magnificence of this sunrise further emphasized the contrast between the calm beauty of the ocean and the island which it surrounded, for the island had the appearance of a place where all civilizations had come to dump their unwanted waste, an elaborate version of a farmer's dung-heap. And this was Ynys Scaith with all its glamors gone, this was what Sactric had called the Empire of Malibann.

The two men rose slowly and stretched painfully, for

their sleep had not been peaceful. Corum flexed first the fingers of his artificial silver hand, then he flexed the fingers of his fleshly hand, which had become so numb it was almost impossible to tell apart from the unnatural one. He straightened his back and groaned, grateful for the wind from the sea which blew away the stink of putrefaction and brought instead a cleansing brine. He rubbed at his eye sockets. The one which lay under the patch itched and seemed a trifle inflamed. He pushed back the patch to let the air get at it, the white, milky scar revealed. Normally he spared himself and others the pain of exposing the wound. Ilbrec had unbraided his golden hair and combed it; now he was plaiting the hair again, weaving in threads of red gold and yellow silver: these braids, thick and strengthened by metal, were the only protection he had for his head, for it was his pride never to fight with a helmet upon his locks.

Then both men walked down to the edge of the sea and washed themselves as best they could in the salt water. The water was cold. Corum could not help wondering if soon it would be frozen. Had the Fhoi Myore already consolidated their victories? Was Bro-an-Mabden now nothing but a dead waste of ice from shore to shore?

"Look," said Ilbrec. "Can you see it, Corum?"

The Vadhagh Prince raised his head but could see nothing on the horizon.

"What did you think you saw, Ilbrec?"

"I can still see it—a sail, I am sure, coming from the direction of Bro-an-Mabden."

"I trust it is not friends bent on our rescue," Corum said miserably. "I would not wish others to fall into this trap."

"Perhaps the Mabden were victorious at Caer Llud," said Ilbrec. "Perhaps we see the first of a squadron of ships armed with Amergin's full magic."

But Ilbrec's words were hollow and Corum could feel no hope. "If it is a ship you see," he said, "I fear it brings further doom to us and those we love." And now he thought he, too, could see a dark sail on the horizon. A ship moving at considerable speed.

"And there—" Ilbrec pointed again—"is that not a second sail?"

Sure enough, for a moment Corum thought he detected another sail, a smaller sail, as if a skiff followed in the wake of the galley, but he did not see it after the first few moments and guessed that it had been a trick of the light.

In trepidation they watched the ship approach. It had a high, curved prow, with a figurehead in the shape of an elongated lion, inlaid with silver, gold and mother-of-pearl. Its oars were shipped and it sailed by the power of the wind alone, its huge black and red sail taut at the mast, and soon there was no question in their minds that it did head for Ynys Scaith. Both Ilbrec and Corum began to shout and yell to the ship, trying to warn it to circumnavigate the island and go on to a more favorable landing place, but its movement was implacable. They saw it go past a promontory and disappear, plainly with the idea of anchoring in the bay. At once, and without ceremony, Ilbrec picked Corum up and placed the Vadhagh upon his shoulders, setting off at a loping pace toward the place where the ship had last been seen. They covered the ground swiftly, for all the debris in their path, and finally Ilbrec arrived, panting, at a natural harbor, in time to see a small boat putting out from the ship, whose sail was now furled.

There were three figures in the boat, but only one, swathed in bulky furs, was rowing. His companions sat in the prow and the stern respectively and they, too, were muffled in heavy capes.

Well before the three men had landed, Ilbrec and Corum had plunged into the sea and were waist-deep, yelling at the tops of their voices.

"Go back! Go back! This is a land of terror!" cried Ilbrec.

"This is Ynys Scaith, the isle of shadows. All mortals who land here are doomed!" Corum warned them.

But the bulky figure continued to row and his companions made no sign that they had heard the shouted words, so that Corum began to wonder if the Malibann had already enchanted the newcomers.

At last Corum and Ilbrec reached the boat itself as it came close to the shore. Corum clung to the side while Ilbrec towered over the boat, looking for all the world like the sea-god his father had been in the legends of the Mabden.

"It is dangerous," boomed Ilbrec. "Can you not hear me?"

"I fear they cannot," said Corum. "I fear they are under a glamor, just as we were."

And then the figure in the prow pushed back his hood and smiled. "Not at all, Corum Jhaelen Irsei. Or, at least, extremely unlikely. Do you not recognize us?"

Corum knew the face well. He recognized the old, handsome features framed by long, grey ringlets and the thick, grey beard; he recognized the hard, blue eyes, the thick, curved lips, the golden collar, inset with jewels, at the throat and the matching jewels on the long, slender fingers. He recognized the warm, mellow voice which was full of a profound wisdom gained at considerable expense of time and mental energy. He recognized the Wizard Calatin whom he had first met in Laahr forest when he had sought the spear, Bryionak, all that long time ago in what seemed to him now to be a happier period of his life.

And at the moment Corum recognized his old enemy Calatin, Ilbrec said in a voice which shook:

"Goffanon! Goffanon!"

For sure enough the bulky figure who had rowed the boat was none other than the Sidhi dwarf, Goffanon of Hy-Breasail, and there was a glassy look in his eyes and his face was slack; but he spoke and said:

"Goffanon serves Calatin again."

"He has you in his power! Oh, I knew that I did not welcome that sail."

Then Corum said urgently: "Even you, Calatin, cannot survive on Ynys Scaith. The people here have enormous powers for the making of lethal illusions. Let

102

us all return to your ship and sail away from here, there to settle our disputes in a pleasanter clime."

Calatin looked around him. He looked at the third figure in the boat who had not revealed his face but kept it thoroughly hidden in his hood. "I find nothing to say against this island," he said.

"It is because you do not see it for what it is," Corum insisted. "Make a bargain, Calatin, to take us back to your ship . . ."

Calatin shook his head and smoothed his grey beard. "I think not. I am tired of sailing. I have never been at my best while crossing water. We shall disembark."

"I warn you, wizard," grumbled Ilbrec, "that the moment you set foot on this land, you are as doomed as all the other wretches who preceded you."

"We shall see. Goffanon, drag the boat high onto the beach so that I shall not wet my garments when I leave the boat."

Obediently Goffanon clambered from the boat and began to haul it through the water and thence onto the beach while Corum and Ilbrec watched helplessly.

Then Galatin stepped elegantly onto the beach and looked around him, stretching his arms so that the surcoat, covered all over in occult symbols, was revealed. He took a deep, appreciative breath of the tainted air, then snapped his fingers, whereupon the other figure, still completely muffled and unrecognizable, rose from the seat in the stern and joined Calatin and Goffanon.

For a moment they stood there, confronting one another with the boat separating them.

"I hope that you are fugitives," said Ilbrec at last. "From the Mabden victory over the Fhoi Myore."

And Calatin smiled and hid his lips with his bejewelled hand.

"Are your Fhoi Myore masters all dead, then . . ." Corum said aggressively, but without much conviction.

"The Fhoi Myore are not my masters, Corum," replied Calatin chidingly, softly. "They are my sometime allies. We work to our mutual advantage."

"You speak as if they are still alive."

"Still alive, aye. They are alive, Corum." Calatin voiced these words in the same controlled tone, his blue eyes full of humor and malice. "And triumphant. And victorious. They hold Caer Llud and now pursue what remains of the Mabden army. Soon all the Mabden will be dead, I fear."

"So we did not win at Caer Llud?"

"Did you expect that you could? Shall I tell you some of those who died there?"

Corum shook his head, turning away, but then he groaned. "Very well, wizard, who died?"

"King Mannach died there, his own battle-standard driven through his body. You knew King Mannach, I believe."

"I knew him. I honor him now."

"And King Fiachadh? Another friend?"

"What of King Fiachadh?"

"He was a prisoner for a few hours, I understand, of my lady Goim."

"Of Goim?" Corum shuddered. He recalled the stories he had heard of the female Fhoi Myore's horrible tastes. "And his son, Young Fean?"

"He shared his father's fate, I believe."

"What others?" whispered Corum.

"Oh, there were many. Many of the Mabden's heroes."

Goffanon said in distant, unnatural tones:

"Ayan the Hairy-handed's friend, the Branch Hero, was torn to pieces by the Hounds of Kerenos, as were Fionha and Cahleen, the warrior-maidens . . .

"And of the Five Knights of Eralskee only the youngest remains alive, if the cold has not taken him by now. He fled on a horse, pursued by Prince Gaynor and the People of the Pines," continued Calatin with relish. "And King Daffyn lost his legs and froze to death not a mile from Caer Llud—he had crawled that mile. We saw his body on our way here. And King Khonun of the Tuha-na-Anu we found hanging from a tree not ten yards from him, discovered by the Ghoolegh we think.

And do you know of one called Kernyn the Ragged, a man of singular dress and unsanitary habits?"

"I know Kernyn the Ragged," said Corum.

"With a group of those he led, Kernyn was found by my lord Balahr's eye and froze to death before he could strike a single blow."

"Who else?"

"King Ghachbes was slain, and Grynion Ox-rider, and Clar from Beyond the West, and the Red Fox, Meyahn, and the two Shamanes, both the Tall and the Short, and Uther of the Melancholy Dale. Also were slain in great numbers warriors of all the Mabden tribes. And Pwyll Spinebreaker was wounded, probably mortally. The same is true of Old Dylann and Sheonan Axe-maiden and perhaps Morkyan of the Two Smiles . . ."

"Stop," said Corum. "Are none of the Mabden left alive?"

"By now I would think it unlikely, though we have traveled for some time. They had little food and were heading for Craig Don, where they could be sure of temporary sanctuary, but they will starve there. They will die at their holy place. Perhaps it is all they want. They know their time upon the earth is over."

"But you are a Mabden," said Ilbrec. "You speak of the race as if it were not your own."

"I am Calatin," said the wizard, as if addressing a child, "and I have no race. Once I had a family, that was all. And the family has gone, too."

"Sent to its deaths on your behalf, as I recall," Corum said savagely.

"They were dutiful sons, if that is what you mean." Calatin laughed lightly. "But I have no natural heirs, it is true."

"And having none of your own, you would see the whole race die?"

"Perhaps that is my motive for doing what I do," agreed Calatin equably. "There again, an immortal has no need of heirs, has he?"

"You are immortal?"

"I hope so."

"By what means did you achieve this?" Corum asked him.

"By the means you know. By choosing my allies properly and using my skills wisely."

"And is that why you visit Ynys Scaith, in the hope of finding more allies, even more despicable than the Fhoi Myore?" said Ilbrec, putting his hand upon the hilt of his sword. "Well, I should warn you that the Malibann have no need of the likes of you and that they will deal with you as they have dealt with us. We have had no luck in convincing them to come to our aid."

"That does not surprise me." Calatin's tone was still equable.

"They will destroy you when they destroy us," said Corum with a certain grim satisfaction.

"I think not."

"Why so?" Ilbrec glowered at the wizard who held his old friend Goffanon in thrall. "Why so, Calatin?"

"Because this is by no means my first visit to Ynys Scaith." He gestured toward the cowled figure on his right. "You said I have no heirs, but it was on Ynys Scaith, with the help of the Malibann, that my son was born. I like to think of him as my son. And it was on Ynys Scaith that I learned many new powers."

"Then it is you!" said Ilbrec. "You are the ally of the Malibann—the one they mentioned."

"I think I must be."

Calatin's smirk was so self-satisfied that Corum drew his sword and ran toward him, but then the flat of Goffanon's axe slammed against his armored chest and he was knocked down onto the filthy beach, while Calatin shook his head in mock despair and said:

"Direct your anger at yourself, Prince Corum of the Silver Hand. You have received poor counsel and followed it. Perhaps if you had been at Caer Llud to lead the Mabden the battle would not have gone so ill . . ."

Corum began to rise, reaching for his sword, which lay a few feet from him, but again black-bearded Goffanon used his axe to push the sword away.

"Prince Corum," said Calatin, "you must know that

the surviving Mabden blame you for their defeat. They call you turncoat. They believe that you joined sides with the Fhoi Myore and fought against them."

"How could they believe that? Now I know you for a liar, Calatin. I was here all the time. What evidence have they?"

Calatin chuckled. "They have good evidence, Prince Corum."

"Then some glamor was put upon them. One of your illusions!"

"Oh, you do me too much honor, Prince Corum."

"Jhary-a-Conel—was he not there?"

"Little Jhary-a-Conel joined with me for a while, when he realized how the battle went, then he vanished —doubtless shamed at his decision, though I considered it sensible."

Then Corum began to weep, feeling even more distressed by the knowledge that his enemy Calatin was witness to this grief.

And as Corum wept a voice came from somewhere. It was Sactric's dry, dead voice and it held a note of impatience.

"Calatin. Escort your company to the Great Palace. We are anxious to see what you have brought us and if you have kept your bargain."

The Fourth Chapter

ON A HILL, BARGAINING FOR THE WORLD'S
FATE

The Great Palace was no longer a palace but a place
where a palace had once been. The huge pine tree which
stood on the very top of Ynys Scaith's only hill had once
grown at the center of the palace, but now there were
only traces of the original foundations. The mortals and
the Sidhi sat upon grass-covered blocks of masonry while
Sactric's mummified figure stood at the spot, where, he
said, their great throne had once rested; this throne, he
had told them, had been carved from a single gigantic
ruby, but none believed him.

"You will see, Emperor Sactric," began Calatin, "that
I have fulfilled the last part of our bargain. I have
brought you Goffanon."

Sactric inspected the expressionless face of the Sidhi
dwarf. "The creature resembles that one whom I desired
to meet again," he admitted. "And he is completely in
your power?"

"Completely." Calatin brandished the little leather
bag which Corum remembered from when he, himself,
had bargained with the wizard. It was the bag into which
Goffanon had spat. It was the bag which Corum had
given to Calatin and whose contents Calatin had used to
secure his power over the great dwarf. Corum looked at
that bag and he was filled with hatred for Calatin even
more intense than he had felt before, but his hatred for
himself was even stronger. With a groan he buried his
face in his hands. Ilbrec cleared his throat and muttered
something, an attempt at comfort, but Corum could not
hear the words.

"Then give me the bag which contains your power."
The decaying hand reached toward Calatin, but Calatin
replaced the little bag in his robe and smiled. "The

power must be transferred willingly, as you know, or it will cease to be. I must first be sure, Sactric, that you will complete that part of the bargain which is yours."

Sactric said bleakly: "We give our word rarely, we of Malibann. When we give it, we are bound to keep it. You requested our help first in destroying what remains of the Mabden race and then in imprisoning the Fhoi Myore in an illusion from which they will be unable to escape, leaving you free to use this world as you feel fit. You have agreed to bring us Goffanon and to help us leave this plane forever. Well, you have brought Goffanon and that is good. We must trust that you have the power to help us depart this world and find another, pleasanter place in which to live. Of course, if you do not succeed in that, we shall punish you. You know this, also."

"I know it, Emperor."

"Then give me the bag."

Calatin showed considerable reluctance to comply as he once more drew out the leather bag, but at last he handed it to Sactric, who accepted it with a hiss of pleasure.

"Now Goffanon, listen to your master Calatin!" Calatin began, while the dwarf's friends looked on in misery. "You have a new master, now. It is this great man, this emperor, this Sactric." Calatin stepped forward and took Goffanon's huge head in his jewelled fingers and turned it so that the eyes stared directly at Sactric. "Sactric is your master now and you will obey him as you have obeyed me."

Goffanon's words were slurred, the speech of an idiot, but they heard him say:

"Sactric is my master now. I will obey him as I have obeyed Calatin."

"Good!" Calatin stepped back with a look of considerable self-importance on his handsome face. "And now, Emperor Sactric, how do you intend to dispose of my two enemies here?" He indicated Corum and Ilbrec. "Would you allow me to devise a means . . . ?"

109

"I am not yet sure I wish to dispose of them," said Sactric. "Why slaughter good animals before they need to be eaten?"

Corum saw Ilbrec pale a little at Sactric's choice of phrase and he, himself, found the words distressing. Desperately, he tried to devise a method of capturing Sactric, at very least, but he knew that Sactric was able to enter and leave his mummified corpse at will and to invoke lethal illusions at a moment's whim. There was little either he or Ilbrec could do but pray that Calatin would not get his will.

Calatin shrugged. "Well, they must die at some time. Corum, in particular . . ."

"I will not discuss the question until I have tested Goffanon." Sactric returned his attention to the Sidhi smith. "Goffanon. Do you remember me?"

"I remember you. You are Sactric. You are now my master," rumbled the dwarf, and Corum groaned to see his old friend brought so low.

"And do you remember that you were once here before, on this island you call Ynys Scaith?"

"I was on Ynys Scaith before." The dwarf closed his eyes and moaned to himself. "I remember. The horror of it . . ."

"But you left again. Somehow you overcame all the illusions we sent you and you went away . . ."

"I escaped."

"But you took something with you. You used it to protect yourself until you could leave. What became of that which you took?"

"I hid it," said Goffanon. "I did not wish to look at it."

"Where did you hide it, dwarf?"

"I hid it." Goffanon's face now had upon it an idiot grin. "I hid it, Lord Sactric."

That thing was mine, as you know. And it must be returned to me. I must have it again, ere we leave this plane. I shall not leave without it. Where did you hide it, Goffanon?"

"Master, I do not remember."

Sactric's voice now had anger in it and almost, Corum thought, desperation. "You must remember!" Sactric wheeled, pointing a finger from which dusty flesh dropped even as he spoke. "Calatin! Have you lied to me?"

Calatin was alarmed. His air of complacency had disappeared to be replaced with a look of anxiety. "I swear to you, Your Majesty. He must know. Even if it is buried in his memory, the knowledge is there!"

Sactric now placed his claw-like hand upon Goffanon's broad shoulder, shaking the dwarf. "Where is it, Goffanon? Where is that which you stole from us?"

"Buried . . ." said Goffanon vaguely. "Buried, somewhere. I put it in safety. There was a charm to ensure that it could never be found again, save by me . . ."

"A charm? What kind of charm?"

"A charm . . ."

"Be more specific, slave!" Sactric's voice was high; it shook. "What did you do with . . . What did you do with that which you stole from me?" It had become plain to Corum that the Emperor of Malibann had no wish to reveal to the others what Goffanon had taken and it began to dawn on the Vadhagh prince that if he listened carefully he might discover some weakness in the apparently invulnerable sorcerer.

Again Goffanon's answer was vague. "I took it away, master. She . . ."

"Be silent!" Sactric wheeled to address Calatin again. The wizard looked ill. "Calatin, upon your word that you would deliver Goffanon to me I helped you make the Karach, I helped you infuse life into it, as you desired, but now I find that you deceived me . . ."

"I swear to you, Lord Sactric, that I did not. I cannot explain the dwarf's inability to answer your questions. He should do all you tell him without hesitation . . ."

"Then you *have* deceived me—and deceived yourself, moreover. Something has died in this Sidhi's brain—your magic has proved unsubtle. Without his secret we cannot leave this plane—would have no desire to leave this plane. Therefore our bargain ends . . ."

"No!" shrieked Calatin, rising, seeing his own terrible death suddenly appearing in Sactric's cold, blazing eyes. "I swear to you—Goffanon has the secret—let me speak to him . . . Goffanon, listen to Calatin. Tell Sactric what he wishes to know . . ."

And Goffanon's voice answered flatly:

"You are not my master now, Calatin."

"Very well," said Sactric. "You must be punished, wizard . . ."

Then, in a panic, Calatin cried out: "Karach! Karach! Destroy Sactric!"

The hooded figure rose swiftly, tearing off its outer robe and drawing a great sword from a scabbard at its belt. And Corum shouted in fear at what he saw.

The Karach had a Vadhagh face. It had a single eye and another covered by a patch. It had a hand which shone like silver and another made of flesh. It wore ornate armor almost exactly the same as Corum's own. It had a conical cap with a peak and engraved over the peak in Vadhagh lettering was a name: "Corum Jhaelen Irsei" which means Corum, the Prince in the Scarlet Robe.

And the Scarlet Robe, Corum's name-robe, flapped on the Karach's body as it strode toward Sactric.

And the Karach's face was alike in every major detail to Corum's.

And Corum knew now why Artek and his followers had accused him of attacking them on Ynys Scaith. And he knew why the Mabden had been deceived into thinking that he fought with the Fhoi Myore against them. And he knew, too, why Calatin had made that bargain with him, long ago, for his name-robe. Calatin had been planning all this for some time.

And looking upon that face that was not his own face Corum shuddered and his veins became cold.

Now Sactric disdained to use his magic against the Karach, the doppelganger (or perhaps his magic was useless against a creature which was already, itself, an illusion), and he cried to his new servant:

"Goffanon! Defend me!"

And obediently the massive dwarf leapt forward to block the Karach's path, his giant axe swinging.

And, fascinated and full of fear, Corum watched the fight, believing that he at last looked upon the 'brother' of the old woman's prophecy, the one whom he had to fear.

Calatin was screaming at Corum: "There! There is the Karach, Corum! There is the one destined to kill you and to take your place. There is my son! There is my heir! There is the immortal Karach!"

But Corum ignored Calatin and watched the battle as the Karach, its face expressionless, its body apparently tireless, aimed blow after blow at Goffanon, who parried with his double-bladed war-axe, the war-axe of the Sidhi. And Corum could see that Goffanon was tiring, that he had been exhausted before he ever reached the island, and that soon the dwarf would fall to the Karach's sword, and it was then that Corum drew his own sword and ran toward his double, while Sactric laughed:

"You hurry to defend me, too, Prince Corum?"

And Corum darted a look of hatred at the corrupt form of the Malibann before he brought his sword, the cross-forged sword which Goffanon had made for him, down upon the shoulder of the Karach and made the thing turn.

"Fight me, changeling!" Corum growled. "It was what you were created to do, was it not?"

And he drove his sword at the Karach's heart, but the creature stepped aside and Corum could not stop his own momentum and the blade went past the Karach's body and then buried itself in flesh, but it was not the Karach's flesh.

It was Goffanon's flesh that the sword found and Goffanon groaned as the blade pierced his shoulder, while Corum gasped in horror at what, inadvertently, he had done. And Goffanon fell back and it must have been that the sword-blade had lodged itself in a bone for the movement of the dwarf's falling wrenched the sword from Corum's hand and left him without weapons so that the Karach, with a terrible fixed grin on its face, a glitter in its single, soulless eye, advanced to slay him.

Ilbrec now drew his own bright blade Retaliator and

came striding to Corum's assistance, but before he could cross the space Calatin rushed past him and began to flee down the hill, having given up any notion of defeating Sactric and plainly hoping to reach his boat before the Malibann realized he had gone.

But Goffanon saw Calatin and he raised his hand to grasp the sword he had made and which now stuck in his shoulder (and still he was careful not to touch the handle) and he wrenched it from the wound and he turned it, poised it, then flung it with great force after the retreating wizard.

The moon-colored sword whistled across the distance between Goffanon and Calatin and the point found the wizard between the shoulder blades.

Calatin continued to run for some moments, apparently unaware that the sword pierced his body. Then he faltered. Then he fell, croaking:

"Karach! Karach! Avenge me. Avenge me, my only heir! My son!"

The Karach turned, its expression softening, searching for the source of those words, its sword falling to its side. At last its eyes found Calatin (who was still not dead but was attempting to get to his knees and crawl on toward the shore and the boat in which, such a short time before, he had sailed in triumph) and Corum felt sure he detected genuine misery in the Karach's expression as it realized the plight of its dying master.

"Karach! Avenge me!"

And the Karach began stiffly to walk down the hill in the wake of its master until it reached the enfeebled Calatin, whose fine, occult robes were now all smeared with his own blood. And from this distance it seemed to Corum that he, himself, paused beside the wizard and sheathed his sword. It was as if he watched a tableau from the past or the future in which he was the main actor; it was as if he dreamed, for he could not bring himself to move as he watched his double, the Karach, the changeling, stoop and look at Calatin's face in puzzlement, wondering why its master groaned and writhed in this way. It reached out to touch the sword

114

which jutted from Calatin's shoulder blades but then it withdrew its hand as if the sword had been hot. Again it seemed puzzled. Calatin was panting out more words to the Karach, words which the onlookers could not hear, and the Karach put its head on one side and listened carefully.

Calatin's dying hands found a rock. Painfully the wizard pulled his body onto the rock and the moon-colored sword was pushed free, falling to the ground. Then the Karach sheathed its own sword and bent to lift its master, its creator, in its arms.

Sactric spoke now, from behind the three who stood on the hill watching this scene. He said:

"Goffanon, I am still your master. Go after the changeling and destroy it."

But Goffanon spoke in a new voice, a voice full of its old, gruff assurance. And Goffanon said:

"It is not yet time to slay the Karach. Besides, it is not my destiny to slay it."

"Goffanon! I command this!" shouted Sactric, holding up the little leathern bag which contained his power over the Sidhi smith.

But Goffanon merely smiled and began to inspect the wound which the sword he had forged himself had made in his shoulder. "You have no right to command Goffanon," he said.

There was a deep bitterness in Sactric's dry, dead voice when he spoke next:

"So I have been fully deceived by that mortal wizard. I shall not allow my judgement to be clouded so again."

Now the changeling Corum was carrying its master to the beach, but it did not walk toward the boat; instead it began to walk directly into the sea so that soon its scarlet robe was lifted on the surface of the water and surrounded both the creature and the dying wizard like so much thick blood.

"The wizard did not deceive you willingly," said Goffanon. "You must know that truth, Sactric. I was no more in his power when I came here than I was in yours. I let him think he commanded me, for I wished to discover if my friends were still alive and if I could help them . . ."

"They'll not live for long," swore Sactric, "and neither will you, for I hate you most deeply, Goffanon."

"I came of my free will, as I said," the dwarf continued, ignoring Sactric's threats, "for I would make the bargain with you that Calatin hoped to make . . ."

"Then you do know where you hid that which you stole?" Hope had returned to Sactric's tone.

"Of course I know. It is not something I could easily forget."

"And you will tell me?"

"If you agree to my conditions."

"If they are reasonable, I will agree."

"You will gain everything you hoped to gain from Calatin, and you will gain it more honorably . . ." said Goffanon. There was a renewed dignity in the dwarf's bearing, for all his wound evidently caused him pain.

"Honor? That's a Mabden conception . . ." began Sactric. Goffanon cut him off, turning to Corum: "You have much to do now, Vadhagh, if you are to make amends for your stupidities. Go, fetch your sword."

And Corum obeyed, his eyes still fixed on his double. The body of the wizard had sunk completely beneath the waves but the head and shoulders of the changeling could still be seen, and Corum saw that head turning to look at him. Corum felt a shock run through him as single eye met single eye. Then the changeling's face twisted and its mouth opened and it let out such a sudden, dreadful howling that Corum was stopped in his tracks just by the stone where his sword lay.

And then the Karach continued on until its head had disappeared under the surface of the sea. For a second or two Corum saw the scarlet surcoat, his name-robe, drifting on the water before it was pulled down and the Karach was gone.

Corum bent and picked up his sword, Goffanon's gift, and he looked at its strange, silvery whiteness, and it was now smeared with his old enemy's blood; but he was glad, for the first time, that he held the sword, and now

116

he knew that he had a name for it, though it was not a noble name, not the name he would have expected to have given it. But it was the right name. He knew it, just as Goffanon had said he would know it when the moment came.

He carried the sword back to the top of the hill where the single pine grew and he lifted the sword toward the sky and he said in a grim, quiet voice:

"I have a name for the sword, Goffanon."

"I know that you have," said the dwarf, his own tone echoing Corum's.

"I call the sword Traitor," said Corum, "for the first blood it drew was from he who forged it and the second blood it drew was from the one who thought he was that man's master. I call my sword Traitor."

And the sword seemed to burn more brightly and Corum felt renewed energy flow through him (had there been another time, another sword like this? Why did the sensation seem familiar?) and he looked at Goffanon and saw that Goffanon was nodding, that Goffanon was satisfied.

"Traitor," said Goffanon, and he laid a large hand against the wound in his shoulder.

Then Ilbrec said, apparently inconsequentially: "Now that you have a named sword, you will need a good horse. They are the first requisites of a war-knight."

"Aye, I suppose they are," said Corum. He sheathed the sword.

Sactric gestured impatiently. "What is the bargain you seek to make with the Malibann, Goffanon?"

Goffanon was still staring at Corum. "An apt name," he said, "but you give it a dark power now, not a light one."

"That must be," said Corum.

Goffanon shrugged and gave his attention to Sactric, speaking practically. "I have what you want and it shall be yours, but you, in turn, must agree to help us against the Fhoi Myore. If we are successful and if our great Archdruid Amergin is still alive, and if we can recover the last of the Mabden treasures which still reside at Caer

117

Llud, then we promise that we shall let you leave this plane and find another better suited to you."

Sactric nodded his mummified head. "If you can keep your bargain, we shall keep ours."

"Then," said Goffanon, "we must work speedily to accomplish the first part of our task, for time runs out for the beleaguered remnants of the Mabden army."

"Calatin spoke the truth?" said Corum.

"He spoke the truth."

Ilbrec said: "But Goffanon, we knew you to be wholly in the wizard's power while he held that bag of spittle. How could it be that you were at no time in his power on your journey here?"

Goffanon smiled. "Because the bag did not contain my spittle . . ." He was about to explain further when Sactric interrupted.

"Do you expect me to accompany you back to the mainland?"

"Aye," said Goffanon. "That will be necessary."

"You know it is hard for us to leave this island."

"But it is necessary," said Goffanon. "At least one of you must come with us and it should be the one in whom all the power of the Malibann is invested—namely yourself."

Sactric thought for a moment. "Then I will need a body," he said. "This one will not do for such a journey." He added: "Best if you are not trying to deceive the Malibann, Goffanon, as you deceived them once before . . ." His tone had become haughty again.

"It is not, this time, in my interest," said the dwarf. "But know you this, Sactric, I have no relish for making bargains with you and, if it were only my decision, I would perish rather than give you back what I stole from you. However the die has been cast so thoroughly that the only way to save the situation now is to continue with what my friends here started. But I think it will go ill for some of us, at least, when your full power is restored to you."

Sactric shrugged his flaking, leathery shoulders. "I would not deny that, Sidhi," he said.

"The question remains," said Ilbrec, "how is Sactric to travel beyond Ynys Scaith if the world outside is inhospitable to him?"

"I need a body." Sactric looked speculatively at the three and caused Corum, at least, to shudder.

"Few human bodies could contain that which is Sactric," said Goffanon. "It is a problem which, for a solution, might require an act of considerable self-sacrifice on the part of one of us . . ."

"Then let that one be me, gentlemen."

The voice was a new one in the company, but it was familiar. Corum turned and saw to his great relief that it was Jhary-a-Conel, as cocky as ever, leaning against a rock with his wide-brimmed hat over one eye and the small, winged, black and white cat on his shoulder.

"Jhary!" Corum rushed forward to embrace his friend. "How long have you been upon the island?"

"I have witnessed most of what has taken place today. Very satisfactory." Jhary winked at Goffanon. "You deceived Calatin perfectly . . ."

"I should not have had the opportunity if it had not been for you, Jhary-a-Conel," said Goffanon. He turned to speak to the others. "It was Jhary who, as soon as it was obvious that the day was going badly for the Mabden, pretended to be a turncoat and offered his services to Calatin who (appreciating his own deviousness and thinking all men like him in that respect) accepted. Thus, by sleight of hand, was Jhary able to substitute the bag containing the spittle for one like it which contained nothing but a little melted snow. Then, to find out what Calatin planned against the Mabden, I had only to pretend to be still in his power, while Jhary lost himself in the general confusion after the retreat from Caer Llud, following discreetly until we came to Ynys Scaith . . ."

"So I did see a smaller sail on the horizon earlier!" said Corum. "It was your skiff, Jhary?"

"Doubtless," said the self-styled Companion to Champions. "And now, as to the other matter, I know that cats have a certain resilience men lack when it comes to containing the souls of other creatures. I remember a time once when my name was different and my circumstances were different, when a cat was used to great effect to contain (and in this case imprison) the soul of a very great sorcerer—but no more of that. My cat will carry you, Sactric, and I think you'll experience little discomfort . . ."

"A beast?" Sactric began to shake his mummified head. "As Emperor of Malibann I could not . . ."

"Sactric," said Goffanon sharply, "you know very well that soon, unless you get free of this plane, you and yours will have perished completely. Would you risk that because of a small point of pride?"

Sactric said savagely: "You speak too familiarly, dwarf. Why, if I were not bound by my word . . ."

"But you are," said Goffanon. "Now, sir, will you enter the cat so that we can leave, or do you not require back that which I took from you?"

"I want it more than life."

"Then, Sactric, you must do as Jhary suggests."

There seemed to be no reaction from Sactric, save that he stared at the black and white cat in some disdain for a moment, then there came a yowling from the cat, its fur stood on end and it clawed at the air before subsiding. And suddenly Sactric's mummy fell heavily to the ground and lay there in a tangled heap.

The cat said:

"Let us go quickly. And remember, I have lost none of my powers merely because I inhabit this body."

"We shall remember," said Ilbrec, picking up the old saddle he had found and dusting it off.

The Sidhi youth, the wounded smith, Goffanon, Corum of the Silver Hand, and Jhary-a-Conel, with that which was now Sactric balancing on his shoulder, began to make their way to the beach and the boat which waited for them.

BOOK THREE

In which Mabden, Vadhagh, Sidhi and
Malibann and the Fhoi Myore struggle
for possession of the Earth herself and
in which enemies become allies and
allies enemies. The Last Battle against
the Cold Folk, against the Frost Eternal.

The First Chapter

THAT WHICH GOFFANON STOLE FROM SAC-
TRIC

The journey had been uneventful, with Ilbrec riding on Splendid Mane and guiding the ship on the shortest course to the mainland. And now they all stood upon a cliff at the foot of which a white, angry sea thundered, and Goffanon raised his double-bladed war-axe high above his head, using his one good arm, and then he drove the axe down into the turf which had, until a few minutes earlier, been marked by a small cairn of stones.

The extraordinarily intelligent eyes of the black and white cat watched Goffanon intensely and sometimes those eyes seemed to burn ruby red.

"Be careful you do not harm it," said the cat in Sactric of Malibann's voice.

"I have still to remove the charm I laid," said Goffanon. Having cut away the turf to expose a patch of earth measuring some eighteen inches across, the Sidhi dwarf knelt over this and ran some of the earth through his fingers, muttering what seemed to be a series of simple, rhymed couplets. When this was done he grunted, took out his knife and began to dig carefully in the soft ground.

"Ugh!" Goffanon found what he sought and his face was screwed up in an expression of considerable disgust. "Here it is, Sactric."

And he withdrew from the ground, by its thin strands of hair, a human head, as mummified as Sactric's own had been, yet having an air not of undeniable femininity but also, strangely, of beauty, though there was nothing evidently beautiful about the severed head.

"Terhali!" sighed the little black and white cat, and now there was plainly adoration in its eyes. "Has he harmed you, my love, my sweet sister?"

And now they all gasped as the head opened eyes

which were pure and clear and icy green. And the rotting lips replied: "I hear your voice Sactric, my own, but I do not see your face. Perhaps I am still a little blind?"

"No, I have had to inhabit this cat for the nonce. But soon we shall be in new bodies, bodies which can accept us, on some other plane. There is a chance that we might escape from this plane at last, my love."

They had brought a casket with them from Ynys Scaith and into this box of bronze and gold they now lowered the head. As the lid closed the eyes stared from the gloom.

"Farewell, for the moment, beloved Sactric!"

"Farewell, Terhali!"

"And that is what you stole from Sactric," murmured Corum to Goffanon.

"Aye, the head of his sister. It is all that is left of her. But it is enough. She has power equal to her brother's. If she had still been on Ynys Scaith when you went there, I doubt you would have survived at all."

"Goffanon is right," said the black and white cat, staring hard at the box which the dwarf now tucked under his arm. "That is why I would not leave this plane until she was restored to me. She is all that I love, Terhali."

Jhary-a-Conel reached up and gave the cat's head a sympathetic pat. "It is what they say, is it not, about even the worst of us having tenderness for something . . ." And he brushed away an imaginary tear.

"And now," said Corum, "we must make haste for Craig Don."

"Which way?" asked Jhary-a-Conel, looking around him.

"That way," said Ilbrec, pointing east, "toward the winter."

Corum had almost forgotten how fierce was the Fhoi Myore winter and he was grateful that they had come upon the abandoned village and found riding horses there, and thick furs to wear, for without both they would now be in a sorry plight. Even Ilbrec was muffled in the pelts of the snow-fox and the marten. Four nights had passed and each night seemed to herald a colder morning. Everywhere they had seen the familiar signs of the Fhoi Myore victories—ground cracked open as if from the blow of a gigantic hammer, frozen bodies twisted in the contours of agony, mutilated corpses of human folk as well as beasts, ruined towns, groups of warriors frozen on the spot by the power of Balahr's eye, children ripped into a dozen pieces by the teeth of the Hounds of Kerenos—the signs of that frightful, unnatural winter which was destroying the very grass of the fields and leaving desolation wherever the ice formed. Through deep drifts of snow they forced their way, falling often, stumbling frequently, and occasionally losing track of their direction altogether—blundering on toward Craig Don, which might already be the graveyard of the last of the Mabden.

And the white snow continued to fall from the gray and endless sky, and their blood felt like ice in their veins, and their skins cracked and their limbs grew stiff and painful so that even breathing hurt their chests and, leading their horses, they were often tempted to lie down in the soft snow and forget their ambitions and die as they knew their comrades must have died.

And at night, when they would light a poor fire and sit close to it, they would scarcely be able to move their lips to speak and it seemed that their minds were as numbed by the cold as their bodies; often the only sound would be the murmur of the small black and white cat as it curled beside the bronze and gold casket and spoke to the head within, and they would hear the head reply, but they would feel no curiosity concerning the nature of the conversation between Sactric and Terhali.

Corum was not sure how many days and nights had passed (he was merely faintly surprised that he was still alive) when they came to the crest of a low hill and looked out across a wide plain over which fell a thin drift of snow; and there in the distance they saw a wall of mist and they recognized the mist for what it was—the mist which went everywhere that the Fhoi Myore went and which some believed was created by their foul breath or which others thought was necessary to sustain the diseased lives of the Cold Folk. And they knew that they had come to the Place of the Seven Stone Circles, the holy place of the Mabden, their greatest Place of Power, Craig Don. And as they rode closer they began to hear the horrid howling of the Hounds of Kerenos, the strange, melancholy booming tones of the Fhoi Myore, the rustlings and whisperings of the Fhoi Myore vassals, the People of the Pines who had once been men but were now brothers to the trees.

"This means," said Jhary-a-Conel, riding close to Corum on a horse which pushed wearily through snow which sometimes came up to its neck, "that some of our comrades still live. The Fhoi Myore would not remain so close to Craig Don unless there was something to keep them here."

Corum nodded. He knew that the Fhoi Myore feared Craig Don and would normally avoid the place at all costs; Gaynor had revealed that when he thought he had trapped them there, months before.

Ilbrec rode ahead on Splendid Mane, driving a path through the snow which the others could follow. If it had not been for the Sidhi giant, their progress would have been much slower and, indeed, it was likely that they would never have reached Craig Don before the cold consumed them. Goffanon went next, on foot as always, his axe over his shoulder, the box containing Terhali's head under his arm. His wound had begun to heal, but the shoulder was still stiff.

"The Fhoi Myore circle is complete," said Ilbrec. "We shall not get through their ranks undetected, I fear."

"Or unscathed." Corum watched his own breath billow white upon the freezing air and he tugged the thick furs tighter to his shivering body.

"Could not Sactric conjure some illusion for us that would allow us to pass through the besiegers without being seen?" Jhary suggested.

Goffanon did not like this suggestion. "It would be best to save the illusions for later," he said, "so that none will suspect the truth when the crucial moment comes . . ."

"I suppose that is wise," agreed Jhary-a-Conel reluctantly. "Then we must make a dash for it, I would say. At least they expect no one to attack them from beyond Craig Don."

"No one in their right mind would," said Corum with a faint smile.

"I do not think we are sane, at present," Jhary replied. And he managed to wink.

"What do you think, Sactric?" Ilbrec asked the black and white cat.

Sactric frowned. "I would rather that my sister and I conserved our strength until the last moment. What you ask of us is considerable, for it is much harder to use our power away from Ynys Scaith."

Ilbrec accepted this. "I will go first to clear the path. Keep close behind me." He drew the great blade Retaliator and it shone strangely in the cold light; it was a thing of the sun and the sun had not been seen on this plain for some long while. Warmth glowed from it and seemed to melt the snowflakes as they fell. And Ilbrec laughed and his ruddy face was full of golden radiance and he cried to his horse:

"On, Splendid Mane! On to Craig Don! On to the Place of Power!"

Then he was galloping so that the snow flew in huge clouds on either side of him and his comrades followed close behind, yelling and waving their weapons, both to sustain their spirits and to keep themselves as warm as possible as Ilbrec vanished first into the unnaturally cold Fhoi Myore mist, leading the way to Craig Don.

Then Corum had also entered the mist, keeping his eyes fixed as closely as he could on his gigantic comrade, and now he had an impression of huge, dark, bulky shapes moving through the mist, of hounds barking warnings, of riders with green-tinged skins trying to detect the nature of those who had suddenly charged into their camp, and he heard a voice he recognized crying:

"Ilbrec! It is the giant! The Sidhi come to Craig Don! Rally Ghoolegh! Rally!"

And it was Prince Gaynor's voice—the voice of Gaynor the Damned, whose fate was so closely linked to Corum's.

Now the hunting horns of the Ghoolegh sounded as they called their fierce dogs to them and the mist was filled with a frightful yapping, yet still Corum could not see the pale beasts with their blood-red ears and their hot, yellow eyes, the beasts which his friend Goffanon feared above all other things.

A huge groaning answered Gaynor's warning, a voice full of pain, and Corum knew that this was the voice of Kerenos himself, wordless, anguished, bleak; the voice of one of the Lords of Limbo, as desolate as the plane from which these dying dogs had originated. Corum hoped that Kerenos' brother, Balahr, was not close by, for Balahr had only to direct his gaze upon them to freeze them for eternity.

Suddenly Corum found his path blocked by four or five slack-faced creatures with skins almost as white as the surrounding snow; creatures armed with thick-bladed flenchers more suitable for hacking the carcasses of game than for fighting, but he knew that these were the favored weapons of the Ghoolegh and it was Ghoolegh he faced now. With his moon-colored sword he sliced about him, astonished at the ease with which the metal slid through flesh and bone, and he realized that the sword had, indeed, attained its full power now that it had been named. And though it was almost impossible to kill the Ghoolegh, he maimed his opponents so badly that they ceased to be any danger to him and he was able to pass easily through their ranks and catch up with Ilbrec who could still be seen ahead, Retaliator rising and falling like living flame and slaying pine-folk and the few hounds who had so far answered the call of the Ghoolegh horns.

For a while, in the exhilaration of battle, Corum was barely aware of the Fhoi Myore mist he breathed, but slowly he realized that his throat and lungs felt as if ice formed solidly in them and his movements were becoming more sluggish, as were the movements of his horse. And desperately he shouted his battle-cry:

"I am Corum! I am Cremm Croich of the Mound! I am Llaw Ereint, the Silver Hand! Tremble, lackeys of the Fhoi Myore, for the Mabden heroes have returned to the Earth! Tremble, for we are the Enemies of Winter!"

And the sword called Traitor flashed and brought cold death to a snapping dog, while elsewhere Goffanon sung a dirge-like song as he whirled his axe with one hand in a circle of deadly metal, and Jhary-a-Conel, the black and white cat clinging to his shoulder, a blade in each hand, struck about him, screaming something which seemed more like a scream of fear than a battle-song.

Now they were closing in from all sides and Corum heard the fearful creaking of the Fhoi Myore battle-carts and knew that Balahr and Goim and the others must be close by and that once the Fhoi Myore found them they would be doomed, but now, too, he could see the shadowy outlines of the first great stone circle of Craig Don—huge, rough-cut pillars which were topped by stone slabs almost as long as those which supported them. And seeing the great Place of Power so close gave Corum the extra strength to force his horse through the green-faced Pine Warriors who rode at him, to hack this way and that with Traitor and draw sap-like blood which filled the air with the cloying stink of the pine-tree. He saw Goffanon, beset by a pack of white hounds, go down on one knee, his black head thrown back, his deep voice roaring his defiance, and he burst into the pack, slicing at a throat here, a belly there, giving Goffanon time to rise and stumble into the sanctuary of the first circle and stand panting with his broad back against a granite pillar. Then Corum himself had reached the circle and was safe and within seconds Ilbrec and Jhary had joined them and they all stood there, grinning at one another, unable to believe that they still lived.

And from beyond the stone circle they heard Prince Gaynor shouting:

"Now we have them all! They will starve as the others starve!"

But the booming, miserable voices of the Fhoi Myore seemed to contain a note of concern, and the howling of the Hounds of Kerenos had an uncertain quality to it, and the Ghoolegh and the Pine Warriors who clustered on the outskirts peered at the four comrades with wary respect, and Corum called back to his old enemy, his brother in destiny:

"Now the Mabden will rally and drive you away forever, Gaynor!"

And Gaynor's voice was amused. "Are you sure they will rally to you, Corum? After you turned against them? I think, my friend, that you will find them reluctant even to speak to you, for all that they are near-dead and you are their only hope . . ."

"I know of Calatin's trick and what he did to destroy the Mabden morale. I will explain this to Amergin."

Gaynor made no further reply in words, but his laughter cut deeper into Corum's spirit than could the sharpest of retorts.

Slowly the four heroes made their way through the archways of the stone circles, passing wounded men and dead men, and mad men, and weeping men, and men who stared unseeingly into space, until at last they came to the central circle where a few tents had been erected and a few fires flickered and men in broken armor, in torn furs, crouched shivering beside their tattered battle banners and waited for death.

Amergin, slender, frail, very proud, stood beside the stone altar of Craig Don where once he had lain after Corum had rescued him from Caer Llud. Amergin had a gloved hand resting upon that altar now as he looked up and recognized the four. His face was grim, but he did not speak. Then another figure emerged from behind the High King—a woman whose red hair fell to below her shoulders. There was a crown on her head and she was clad in heavy chain mail from throat to ankle, a heavy, bronze-buckled belt around her waist, a fur cloak on her back. And her eyes burned green and fierce as she looked with contempt upon Corum. It was Medhbh.

Corum made a movement toward her, murmuring: "Medhbh, I have brought . . ."

But her voice was colder than Fhoi Myore mist as she drew herself up, her hand upon the golden pommel of her sword, and said:

"Fiachadh is dead. It is Queen Medhbh now. I am Queen Medhbh and I lead the Tuha-na-Cremm Croich. Under our High King, Amergin, I lead all the Mabden, those who are not already slain as a result of your monstrous treachery."

"I did not betray you," said Corum simply. "You were tricked by Calatin."

"We saw you, Corum . . ." began Amergin gently.

"You saw a changeling—you saw a Karach created by Calatin for the very purpose of making you think me a traitor."

"It is true, Amergin," said Ilbrec. "We all saw the Karach, on Ynys Scaith."

Amergin raised his hand to his temple. It was plain that even that movement cost him dear. He sighed. "Then we must have a trial," he said, "for that is the Mabden way."

"A trial?" Medhbh smiled. "At this time?" She turned her back on Corum. "He has proven himself guilty. Now he tells incredible lies; he thinks we are so dazed by defeat that we will believe them."

"We fight for our beliefs, Queen Medhbh," said Amergin, "just as much as we fight for our lives. We must continue to conduct our affairs according to those beliefs. If we do not, then we have no justification for living. Let us question these people fairly and listen to their answers before we judge them innocent or guilty."

Medhbh shrugged her beautiful shoulders. And Corum knew agony then. He knew that he loved Medhbh more than he had ever loved her before.

"We shall find Corum guilty," she said. "And it will be my pleasure to deliver the sentence."

THE YELLOW STALLION

There was hardly a man or woman there who could stand unaided. Gaunt, frozen, half-starved faces looked upon Corum and, for all that they were familiar faces, he saw no sympathy in them; all judged him a turncoat and blamed him for the huge losses they had sustained at Caer Llud. And beyond the seventh circle of stones, the outer circle, the unnatural mist swirled and the bleak voices of the Fhoi Myore boomed and echoed and the Hounds of Kerenos maintained a constant howling. And Corum's trial began.

"Perhaps I was mistaken in seeking allies on Ynys Scaith," commenced Corum, "and thus I am guilty of poor judgement. But of all else, I am innocent."

Morkyan of the Two Smiles, who had only been slightly wounded at Caer Llud, drew his dark brows together and fingered his moustache. His scar was white against his swarthy skin. "We saw you," said Morkyan. "We saw you riding side by side with Prince Gaynor, with the Wizard Calatin, with that other traitor Goffanon—all riding together, leading the Pine Warriors, the Ghoolegh, the Hounds of Kerenos against us. I saw you cut down Grynion Ox-rider and one of the sisters, Cahleen, daughter of Milgan the White, and I heard that you were directly responsible for the death, also, of Phadrac-at-the-Crag-at-Lyth, that you lured him to his death when he thought you still fought for us . . ."

Hisak, nicknamed Sunthief, who had helped Goffanon forge Corum's sword, growled from where he sat with his back against the altar, his left leg in splints, "I saw you kill many of our people, Corum. We all saw you."

"And I say that it was not me whom you saw," Corum insisted. "We came to help. We have been on Ynys Scaith all this time—under a glamor which made us think a few hours had passed when really months had passed . . ."

Medhbh's laughter was harsh. "A folk tale! We cannot believe such childish lies!"

Corum said to Hisak Sunthief: "Hisak, do you remember the sword that the one supposed to be me carried? Was it this sword?"

And he drew forth his moon-colored blade and strange, pale light pulsed from it.

"Was it this sword, Hisak?"

And Hisak shook his head. "Of course it was not. I should have recognized that sword. Was I not present at the ceremony?"

"You were. And if I had a sword of such power, would I have not used it in battle?"

"Probably . . ." admitted Hisak.

"And look!" Corum held up his silver hand. "What is that metal?"

"It is silver, of course."

"Aye! Silver! And did this other—this Karach—did it have a hand of silver . . . ?"

"I recall now," said Amergin, frowning, "that the hand did not seem to be exactly silver. More some kind of mock silver . . ."

"Because silver is deadly to the changeling!" said Ilbrec. "All know that!"

"This is merely a complicated deception," said Medhbh, but she was no longer so sure in her accusations.

"But where, then, is this changeling now?" said Morkyan of the Two Smiles. "Why does one vanish and another appear? If we saw both together we could be more easily convinced."

"The Karach's master is dead," said Corum. "Goffanon slew him. The Karach took Calatin into the sea. It was the last we saw of both. We have already fought this changeling, you see."

Corum looked from weary face to weary face and he saw that the expressions were changing. Most were at least prepared to listen to him now.

"And why did you all return," said Medhbh, pushing back her long red hair, "when you knew that the position was hopeless here?"

"What could we gain by aiding you? Is that what you mean?" said Jhary-a-Conel.

Hisak pointed a finger at Jhary. "I saw you riding with Calatin, also. Ilbrec is the only one here who was not evidently in league with our enemies."

"We returned," said Corum, "because we had achieved the object of our quest to Ynys Scaith and brought you aid."

"Aid?" Amergin looked hard at Corum. "Of the kind we discussed."

"Of exactly that kind." Corum indicated the black and white cat and the bronze and gold casket. "Here it is . . ."

"It does not take the form I expected," said Amergin.

"And there is this . . ." Ilbrec was dragging something from one of his panniers. "Doubtless brought in some ship wrecked upon the shores of Ynys Scaith. I recognized it at once." And he displayed the cracked, ancient saddle he had found on the beach.

Amergin sighed with surprise and stretched his hands towards the saddle. "I know it. It is the last of our treasures to remain unlocated, save for the Collar and the Cauldron, which still reside in Caer Llud."

"Aye," said Ilbrec, "and doubtless you know the prophecy attached to this saddle?"

"I do not recall any definite prophecy," Amergin said. "I was always puzzled as to why such an evidently useless old saddle was included in our treasures."

"It is Laegaire's saddle," said Ilbrec. "Laegaire was my uncle. He died in the last of the Nine Fights. He was half-mortal, you'll recall . . ."

"And he rode the Yellow Stallion," said Amergin, "which could only be ridden by one who was pure in spirit and who fought in a just cause. So that is why this saddle has been preserved with our other treasures."

"That is why. But I do not mention all this merely in order to pass the time. I know how to call the Yellow

133

Stallion. And thus I might have the means of proving to you that Corum does not lie. Let me call the Stallion, then let Corum try to ride the beast. If it accepts him, then you will know that he is pure in spirit and that he fights in a just cause—your cause."

Amergin looked at his companions. "This seems fair," said the High King.

Only Medhbh was reluctant to accept Amergin's judgement. "It could be a sorcerous trick," she said.

"I will know if it is," said Amergin. "I am Amergin. Forget not that, Queen Medhbh."

And she accepted her High King's rebuke and turned away.

"Let a space be cleared near the altar," said Ilbrec, carrying the saddle carefully to the great stone slab and placing it thereon.

They stood away from the altar, on the fringes of the first circle of monoliths, and they watched as Ilbrec turned his golden head toward the cold sky and spread his huge arms so that what little light there was gleamed on his red gold bracelets, and Corum was suddenly impressed anew of the power emanating from this noble, barbaric god, the son of Manannan.

And Ilbrec began to chant:

In all nine great fights did Laegaire struggle.
Small though he was, his bravery was huge.
No Sidhi fought better and none more cunningly
For the Mabden cause.

Laegaire was his name, of undying honor,
Famous for his humility, he rode the Yellow Steed,
And led the charge at Slieve Gullion,
Though few warriors then remained.

The day was won, but Goim's javelin had found him,
And Laegaire lay in warm, wet crimson,
His head upon his saddle, dying a warrior's death,
While his yellow horse wept.

134

Few were left to hear it when Laegaire named his heir,
Calling to the oak and alder as witness,
Saying that he had owned nothing but life and his steed;
His life he gave willingly to the Mabden.

To the Yellow Stallion Laegaire granted freedom,
Making only one condition on him:
If again Old Night threatened, he must return
And a pure Champion serve in the Mabden cause.

So, dying, Laegaire told his witnesses to take his saddle,
A reminder of his noble oath,
Saying that he who could sit in it would prove true,
That the Yellow Stallion would know him.

In summer fields the Stallion grazes,
Awaiting Laegaire's heir;
Now in Laegaire's name we call him;
To charge again upon Old Night.

And now Ilbrec sank upon his knees before the altar
on which the old, cracked saddle stood, and his last
words were uttered in what was almost an exhausted
sigh.

Save from the noises in the distance, the boomings and
the howlings, there was silence. None moved. Ilbrec remained where he was, his head lowered. They waited.

And then there came a new sound from somewhere,
but none could tell from which direction, whether from
above them or below, but it was the unmistakeable
sound of a horse's hooves galloping closer. This way and
that they looked, but nowhere could they see the horse,
yet still it came closer until it seemed to be within the
stone circle. They heard a snorting, a high, proud
whinnying, the stamping of metal shod hooves on frozen
ground.

Then suddenly Ilbrec lifted his head and laughed.

And a yellow horse stood there on the other side of
the altar, an ugly horse which yet had nobility in its

bearing and a look of warm intelligence in its marigold-colored eyes. Its breath poured from its flared nostrils and it tossed its mane and it looked expectantly at Ilbrec, who got slowly from his knees and picked the saddle up in his two huge hands and placed it gently upon the back of the Yellow Stallion, and patted the beast's neck, and spoke to it lovingly, mentioning Laegaire's name frequently.

Ilbrec turned, gesturing toward Corum:

"Now, Corum, try to mount the horse. If he accepts you it will prove to all that you can be no betrayer of the Mabden."

Hesitantly, Corum stepped forward. At first the Yellow Stallion snorted and backed away, flattening its ears against its head, studying Corum with those intelligent eyes.

Corum put a hand upon the pommel of the saddle and the Yellow Stallion turned its head to inspect him, sniffing him. Corum climbed carefully into the saddle and the Yellow Stallion lowered its long head to the ground and unconcernedly began to nose about in the snow for grass. It had accepted him.

So now the Mabden cheered him, calling him Cremm Croich, Llaw Ereint, and the Hero of the Silver Hand, their Champion. And Medhbh, who was now Queen Medhbh, came forward with tears in her eyes, stretching out her soft hand to Corum but saying nothing. And Corum took her hand, bent his head and kissed her hand with his lips.

"And now we must consult," said Goffanon, his voice brisk. "What are we to do against the Fhoi Myore?" He stood beneath one of the arches, resting his hand upon the haft of his axe, and he stared beyond the stone circles of Craig Don into a mist which appeared to be thickening.

Sactric, in the form of the black and white cat, spoke in a quiet, dry tone. "Ideally, I would gather, it would suit you if the Fhoi Myore were where you are now and you were elsewhere . . ."

Amergin nodded. "That is assuming that the Fhoi

136

Myore have real reason to avoid Craig Don. If it is merely a superstition, then we are lost."

Sactric said: "I do not think it merely superstition, Amergin. I, too, understand the power of Craig Don. I must consider how best I can help you, but I must have your assurance that you, in turn, will help me if I am successful on your behalf."

"Once I have the Collar of Power again," said the Archdruid, "I can help you. Of that I am certain."

"Very well, you have made the bargain." Sactric seemed satisfied.

"Aye," said Goffanon grimly from where he stood, "we have made the bargain."

Corum looked enquiringly at his friend, but the Sidhi dwarf would say no more.

Medhbh whispered in Corum's ear as he dismounted: "I thought I would not be able to do this, but now I know that I was mistaken, there is a charm I have which will help you, of that I have been assured."

"A charm?"

She said: "Give me that hand of silver for a little while. I have the means to make it stronger than it is."

He smiled. "But Medhbh, I need no extra strength . . ."

"You will need everything anyone can give in the coming struggle," she insisted.

"Where did you get this charm?" To humor her he began to take out the little pins which secured the hand to his wrist stump. "From an old wise woman?"

She evaded answering him. "It will work," she said. "I have been promised that."

He shrugged and handed her the beautifully wrought silver thing. "You must let me have it back soon," he said, "for it will not be long before I go to do battle with the Fhoi Myore."

She nodded. "Soon, Corum." And she darted at him a look of considerable affection so that again his heart was lightened and he was able to smile. Then she took his silver hand into her small tent of skins, to the left of the altar, while Corum discussed the problems of the moment with Amergin, Ilbrec, Goffanon, Jhary-a-Conel, Morkyan of the Two Smiles, and the other remaining Mabden war-knights.

By the time Medhbh had returned and given Corum back the metal hand, offering him a reassuring and significant glance, they had determined what their best course of action would be.

With Terhali's help, Sactric would conjure a vast illusion, to transform Craig Don into a form which the Fhoi Myore would not fear, but before that could be engineered, the Mabden must risk the few warriors they had left in a final attack upon the Cold Folk and their vassals.

"We take a considerable risk," said Amergin, watching Corum strap the silver hand back upon his wrist, "and we must be prepared for the possibility that none of us will survive. We might all be dead before Sactric and Terhali can keep their part of our bargain."

And Corum looked at Medhbh and he saw that she loved him again, and the prospect of dying saddened him then.

The Third Chapter

THE STRUGGLE AGAINST OLD NIGHT

And now they went, for the last time, upon the Fhoi Myore, and they were proud in their ragged armor and they carried their shredded standards high. Chariots moaned as their wheels began to turn; horses stamped upon the ground and snorted, and the booted feet of marching men began to thump like the beating of a martial drum. Pipes skirled, fifes wailed, tabors rattled, and all that remained of the Mabden strength poured out of the sanctuary of Craig Don to do battle with the Cold Folk.

And all that remained, perched upon the old stone altar, were a small black and white cat and a box of bronze and gold.

Corum led them, riding the Yellow Stallion, the moon colored sword Traitor in his hand of flesh, a round war-board upon his left arm, and two javelins in his silver hand (with which he also held the reins of the yellow steed). And Corum felt the power and the confidence of the horse he rode and he was glad. And on one side of Corum rode the High King, the Archdruid Amergin, disdaining armor and clad in flowing robes of blue over which were draped furs of ermine and the skin of the winter doe, and on the other side of Corum rode the proud Queen Medhbh, all in stiff armor, her crown upon her shining helm, her red hair flowing free and mingling with the heavy furs of the bear and the wolf, her sling at her belt and her sword in her hand; she smiled once at Corum before he had ridden past the last stone circle and into the thickness of the mist, calling:

"Fhoi Myore! Fhoi Myore! Here is Corum come to destroy you!"

And the Yellow Stallion opened its ugly mouth and displayed discoloured teeth and from its curling lips there issued a peculiar noise that was like nothing but defiant, sardonic laughter, and then it leapt forward suddenly and it was plain its marigold-colored eyes could see easily through the mist, for it carried Corum surely toward his enemies, as it had carried its old master Laegaire into the last and ninth of his fights, at Slieve Gullion.

"Hai, Fhoi Myore! You'll not hide for long in your mist!" Corum called, drawing his fur collar around his mouth to keep out as much of the cold as he could.

For a moment he saw a huge, dark shape looming close by, but then it had gone again, and then he heard the familiar creak of wicker, the shambling sounds of the Fhoi Myore's malformed beasts of burden, and then he heard soft laughter that was not Fhoi Myore laughter, and he turned and he saw what at first appeared to be a fire flickering, but it was the armor of Prince Gaynor the Damned, glowing crimson and yellow and then scarlet, and behind Gaynor rode a score of Pine Warriors, their pale green faces set, their green eyes glaring, their green bodies astride green horses. Corum turned to face them, hearing Ilbrec's voice shouting to Goffanon from another part of the field:

"Beware, Goffanon, it is Goim!"

But Corum could not see how Ilbrec and Goffanon fared against the horrid female Fhoi Myore, and he had no time to call out, for now Prince Gaynor came charging down, and he heard only the old, familiar note of the horn which Goffanon blew again to confuse the Ghoolegh and the Hounds of Kerenos.

The Arms of Chaos, the eight-arrowed sign, burned bright on Gaynor's breastplate as he charged, and the sword in his hand shifted its colors from gold to silver and then to sky-blue, while Gaynor's bitter laughter sounded from behind his featureless helm and he sang out:

"Now I face you at last, Corum, for this is the time!"

And Corum raised his round shield and Gaynor's flickering sword bit hard into the silver rim and Corum struck with his own moon-colored sword Traitor at Gaynor's helm and Gaynor yelled as the blade almost pierced the metal.

Gaynor dragged his sword free and hesitated. "You have a new sword, Corum?"

"Aye. It is called Traitor. Is it not fine, Gaynor?" Corum laughed, knowing his old enemy to be disconcerted.

"I do not think it is your destiny to defeat me in this fight, brother," said Gaynor thoughtfully.

Elsewhere Medhbh was engaged with half a score of Ghoolegh, but was giving a good account of herself, Corum saw, before the mist obscured her again.

"Why call me brother?" Corum said.

"Because our fates are so closely linked. Because we are what we are . . ."

And Corum wondered again if the old woman's prophecy had referred to Gaynor as the one he must fear. Fear beauty, she had said, fear a harp, and fear a brother . . .

And with a yell Corum urged his laughing horse at Gaynor, and Traitor struck again and seemed to pierce the armor protecting Gaynor's shoulder so that Gaynor shrieked and his armor burned an angry crimson. Thrice he struck back at Corum while the Vadhagh Prince tried to dislodge his sword from Gaynor's shoulder, but all three blows landed on Corum's shield and succeeded only in numbing Corum's arm.

"I like this not," said Gaynor. "I knew nothing of a sword called Traitor." But then he seemed to pause and speak in a different, more hopeful tone. "Would it kill me, do you think, Corum?"

Corum shrugged. "You must ask Goffanon the Sidhi smith that question. He forged the blade."

But Gaynor was already turning his horse about, for Mabden with brands had emerged from the mist and with fire were driving the Pine Warriors back, for that part of the warriors that was brother to the tree feared fire above all else. And Gaynor called to his men to rally, to press the attack against the Mabden, and soon he was lost in the midst of the Pine Warriors, once more abdicating from a direct conflict with Corum, for Corum was the only mortal who could fill Gaynor the Damned with terror.

And for an instant Corum found himself alone, knowing not where his enemies lurked or where his friends were, but hearing the sounds of battle all around him in the chilling mist.

And then from behind him he heard a small groaning noise which grew until it became a sort of bleat, and then a deep, melancholy honking, at once stupid and menacing, and Corum remembered that voice and knew that Balahr sought him, remembering how Corum had once wounded him. And he heard the creaking of a great wicker battle-cart, and there came to his nostrils the stink of sickness, the odor of diseased flesh, and he controlled his wish to flee away from the source of that stink, and he readied himself at last to face the Fhoi Myore. The Yellow Stallion reared once, its hooves lashing at the air, then became quiet and tense, watching the mist with its warm, intelligent eyes.

Corum saw a black shape approaching; it moved with a lurching, unsteady gait as if two legs on one side were shorter than the others; large, blubbery lumps jutted from its body and its head lolled as if its neck had been snapped. Corum saw a red, toothless mouth, watery eyes set asymmetrically on the left side of its head, blue-green nostrils blowing shreds and scraps of leathery skin with every exhalation as, painfully, it dragged its master's chariot behind it. And in the chariot, steadying itself by means of one grotesque arm braced against the wicker wall, its body all covered in a kind of wiry, matted fur spotted with patches of something resembling the mold which grows on decaying food, with patches of bare skin bearing a form of flaking yellow eczema, stood Balahr, booming out his insensate anger. And Balahr's face was red, as if something had chewed it, and there were sores on it and pieces of raw flesh on it, and in places the bones showed through it, for Balahr, like his fellows, was slowly dying of a dreadful, rotting disease, the result of

142

their inhabiting this alien plane for too long. And on Balahr's left cheek something opened and closed and it was Balahr's mouth, and, above the mouth and the eaten-away nose, there was a single huge lid of dead flesh covering Balahr's terrible, freezing eye, and from the eyelid there ran a wire secured to the flesh by a great hook, and the wire had been passed over Balahr's skull and under his arm pit and the end of the wire was held in Balahr's hand, his two-fingered hand.

The honking became more agitated, the head turned, seeking out Corum and Corum thought he heard his own name issue from Balahr's lips, he thought they formed the word "Corum," but he guessed that this was his imagination.

Then, without Corum's urging, the Yellow Stallion leapt forward, even as Balahr began to move his hand to open his single eye. The horse jumped and it was on one side of the giant, immediately below it, and Corum was able to swing himself from his saddle and take hold of the side of the cart and drag himself up and plunge the first of his javelins deep into the rotting flesh of Balahr's groin.

Balahr grunted in surprise and began to feel around for the source of the pain. Corum drove the second javelin as hard as he could into Balahr's chest.

Balahr found the first javelin and plucked it out, but he plainly had not noticed the second. Again he began to tug at the wire which would open his lethal eye.

And Corum jumped and took hold of a handful of Balahr's wiry hair, clambering up the giant's thigh, almost losing his grip as the hair was wrenched free from the flesh and Balahr shook himself, just as Corum plunged his sword into the Fhoi Myore's back and clung on to the hilt, swinging, for a moment, free in the air.

Balahr snorted and honked, but kept his two-fingered hand upon the wire which would open his eye, slapping at his back with his other hand, and Corum managed to get another purchase in the hair and began to climb again.

Balahr swayed in the chariot and the beast which

dragged the chariot seemed to interpret this as a signal to move so that suddenly Balahr was swaying and the chariot was moving and the Fhoi Myore was almost flung backwards from the platform but, with one awkward movement, was able to steady himself again.

And Corum scrambled higher up the back, choking on the stink of the diseased flesh, until he reached the wire at the point where it ran under Balahr's armpit. And then Corum raised his sword Traitor and he hacked at the wire. Once, twice, thrice, he hacked, while Balahr honked and swayed and blew out huge clouds of foul, misty breath, and then the wire was severed.

But with the wire broken Balahr had two hands free and he used them to find Corum so that suddenly Corum was engulfed by a great, crushing fist and his arms were trapped so that he could not use his moon-colored sword.

And then Balahr grunted and lowered his head and Corum, looking down also, saw that the Yellow Stallion was there, lashing at Balahr's misshapen legs with its hooves.

The Fhoi Myore was not intelligent enough to concentrate on both Corum and the horse and it began to bend, groping for its new attacker, his grip on Corum weakening so that the Vadhagh Prince was able to struggle free, hacking at the fingers as he did so. One finger fell to the ground and sticky ichor began to ooze from the wound, and then Corum was falling, to land flat on his back, all the breath knocked from him. Painfully he got up and he saw that the Yellow Stallion stood near him and there was humor in its eyes. And Balahr's battle-cart was creaking and moving off into the mist again, its occupant honking in a strange, high tone which, at that moment, filled Corum with a feeling of deep sympathy for the creature.

He got back into the saddle, wincing as he realized to what extent he had been bruised by his fall, and at once the Yellow Stallion was galloping again, passing shadowy groups of fighting men, the monstrous shapes of the Fhoi Myore. He saw horns glinting high above him; he saw a face which resembled a wolf's, he saw white teeth, and he knew that this was the chief of the Fhoi Myore, Kerenos, howling like one of his own hounds and striking about him with a huge, crude sword, striking at an attacker who sang a wild, beautiful song as he fought, whose golden hair shone like the sun, who rode a massive black horse which was clad in red and gilded leather and sea-ivory and pearls. It was Ilbrec, son of Manannan, on his horse Splendid Mane, his shining sword Retaliator in his hand, doing battle with Kerenos, as his Sidhi ancestors had done battle in the old times when they had answered the Mabden call for help and ridden to rid this world of Chaos and Old Night. And then Corum had gone past them, glimpsing Goim, with her hag's face and her filed teeth, snatching with clawed hands at the black-bearded dwarf Goffanon, who yelled at her as he whirled his axe, and hurled insults at the gigantic crone.

Corum wanted to stop, to aid his old comrades, but the Yellow Stallion bore him onward to a place where Queen Medhbh stood over the corpse of her own horse and lashed out at half-a-dozen red-eared hounds who surrounded her. Into these rode Corum, bending low in his saddle and slitting open the bellies of two of the beasts without pausing, calling out to the woman he loved:

"Climb up behind me, Medhbh! Hurry!"

And Queen Medhbh did as he bid her and the Yellow Stallion did not seem to notice the extra weight at all but opened its mouth to laugh again at the hounds snapping all around him.

And then all at once the mist was gone and they were in an oak wood and each oak flamed with a fire which had no heat, a fire of intense brightness, illuminating the battle and making all those who fought lower their weapons and gape, and there was no snow to be seen anywhere.

And five monstrous figures, in five rudely-made chariots drawn by five grotesque beasts, covered their malformed heads and wailed in pain and fear.

For all he guessed the origin of the enchantment,

Corum felt alarm growing within him, and he turned in his saddle and he held Medhbh close, and he was overwhelmed by a profound sense of misgiving.

Now the Fhoi Myore vassals milled about in confusion, looking to their leaders for guidance, but the Fhoi Myore themselves honked and groaned and shuddered, for the combination of oak-tree and fire was probably what they feared most upon this plane.

Goffanon came limping up, using his axe to help him walk. His body bled from a dozen long wounds he had got from Goim's claws, but that was not the reason his face was so grim.

"Well," he growled, "Sactric conjures no arbitrary glamor. Oh, how I fear that knowledge of his."

And Corum could only nod his agreement.

The Fourth Chapter

THE POWER OF CRAIG DON

"Once such a strength of illusion is introduced into a world," said Goffanon, "then it is hard to be rid of it. It will cloud the Mabden minds for many millennia to come. I know that I am right."

Queen Medhbh laughed at him. "I think you relish gloomy thoughts, old smith. Amergin will help the Malibann and that will be an end to it. Our world will be rid of all her enemies!"

"There are subtler enemies," said Goffanon, "and the worst of all is that unreality which mars clear-sighted judgement of things as they are."

But Medhbh shrugged and dismissed his words, pointing to where the Fhoi Myore were urging their chariots away from the conflict, seeking to escape the flaming oaks. "There! Our enemies flee!"

Ilbrec came riding up, his face all flushed, his fair skin bearing the marks of the fight. He laughed. "We did well, after all, to seek help on Ynys Scaith!"

But neither Corum nor Goffanon answered him and so Ilbrec rode on, leaning over in his saddle and chopping casually at the heads of Pine Warriors and Ghoolegh as he went by. None attacked him, for the Fhoi Myore vassals were too confused.

Then, as Medhbh dismounted from the Yellow Stallion and went to catch a horse she had observed nearby, Corum saw Prince Gaynor the Damned riding through the burning oak-wood toward him and, about thirty feet away, Prince Gaynor drew rein.

"What's this?" he asked. "Who aids you, Corum?"

"It would be unwise to tell you, Gaynor the Damned, I think," replied Corum.

He heard Gaynor sigh. "Well, all you have done is to make another sanctuary for yourselves, like Craig Don.

We shall wait on the edges of this place and you will begin to starve again. What have you gained?"

"I do not know, yet," said Corum.

Prince Gaynor turned and began to ride away, in the wake of the disappearing Fhoi Myore. And now the Ghoolegh, the Hounds of Kerenos, the Pine Warriors—all those vassals who still survived—began to stream after Prince Gaynor.

"What now?" said Goffanon. "Shall we follow?"

"At a distance," said Corum. His own men were beginning to regroup. Scarce a hundred remained. Among them were Amergin, the High King, and Jhary-a-Conel, who had a wounded side. His face was very pale and there was agony in his eyes. Corum went to him, inspecting the wound.

"I have put a salve on it," said Amergin, "but he needs better treatment than I can minister here . . ."

"It was Gaynor," said Jhary-a-Conel. "I did not see him in the mist, until too late."

"I owe Gaynor much," said Corum. "Would you wait here or ride with us, after the Fhoi Myore?"

"If their end is to come, I would witness it," said Jhary.

"So be it," said Corum.

And they all began to follow the retreating Fhoi Myore.

So anxious were the Fhoi Myore and their followers to depart the burning oak-wood that they did not see Corum and the Mabden behind them. The only one who looked back and seemed evidently puzzled was Gaynor. Gaynor did not fear the oaks, he feared only Limbo.

Something brushed Corum's shoulder and then he felt a small body settle there. It was the black and white cat and Sactric's eyes stared out from its head.

"How far does this enchantment extend?" Corum asked the Malibann.

"As far as necessary," Sactric told him. "You will see."

"Where is Craig Don? I did not know we had strayed so far from it," Medhbh said.

But Sactric did not answer. He spread his borrowed wings and flew away again.

Amergin was staring hard at the burning oaks. He had a look of respect upon his pale features. "Such a simple-seeming illusion," he murmured, "but what power it took to conceive it. I know now why you feared the Malibann, Goffanon."

Goffanon merely grunted.

A little later the Sidhi dwarf said: "I still cannot rid myself of the thought that it would be better for the Mabden to die now. Your descendants will suffer as a result of the allies you have used today."

"I hope not, Goffanon," said the Archdruid, but he frowned, considering the dwarf's words.

And then Corum saw something, a shadow behind the flaming oaks. He stared hard at it and it began to dawn on him what it was he saw.

Ahead, the Fhoi Myore had come to a halt. Their honkings and their boomings had become still more agitated. They lifted their diseased heads, calling to one another, and there was something pathetic and childlike about their voices.

Corum felt a wave of dizziness sweep through him as he noticed more of the tall shadows. He said:

"It is Craig Don. The Malibann have disguised it. The Fhoi Myore have entered the stone circles!"

And Jhary cried: "My cat! Is Sactric still there?" And the little Companion to Champions spurred his horse forward, heedlessly dashing toward where the Fhoi Myore gathered. Corum realized that the pain of the wound had affected his friend's mind and he shouted: "Jhary! Sactric will protect himself!"

But Jhary did not hear Corum. Already he had reached the nearest group of Pine Warriors and passed them unhindered. Corum made to follow him, but the Yellow Stallion refused to move. Corum kicked his heels into the steed's flanks, but nothing he could do would make the Yellow Stallion take one step closer.

And now it seemed to Corum that the stone circles were whirling around him, and as they whirled the burning oak trees began to disappear, and the cold sky returned, and the white plain, and the mist, and he was half-blinded. They were still within the outer circle of monoliths, but the Fhoi Myore were at the very center. And something seemed to be trying to pull Corum into that inner ring, and a powerful wind tugged at him, but the Yellow Stallion held its ground and Corum clung to the saddle, noticing that many of the Mabden had thrown themselves flat upon the frosty earth.

And Corum heard a terrible grunting and he saw that the Fhoi Myore were trying to burst free from the inner circle, but that the wind forced them back.

"Jhary!" Corum called, but the wind stole his voice. "Jhary!"

Faster and faster the stones whirled and now only Corum remained in his saddle. Even Ilbrec kneeled beside Splendid Mane, close to where Goffanon stood, staring bleakly at the scene taking place at the center of Craig Don.

Corum saw something crimson fling itself clear from the circle and he saw that it was Gaynor the Damned, fighting fiercely against the wind, moving with painful slowness toward the group of Mabden, sometimes falling down, but always managing to rise, his armor flickering with a thousand different colors.

Corum thought: *"So you seek to escape your fate, Gaynor. Well, I shall not allow it. You must go to Limbo."*

And he drew his moon-colored sword Traitor. And the sword pulsed like a live thing in his hand. And he made to block Gaynor's path.

But the wind still dragged at him and, unlike Prince Gaynor, Corum was not motivated by panic, so that when he dismounted from the Yellow Stallion to step in front of Gaynor he was almost knocked from his feet, but nonetheless he flung himself upon his old enemy, grappling clumsily with him.

Gaynor raised a metal fist and smashed it into Corum's face, at the same time wrenching Traitor from

Corum's hand. He raised the sword to strike the Vadhagh Prince down, his armor glowing blue-black, while all around him the stones of Craig Don whirled faster.

Then Corum saw Goffanon come up behind Gaynor and seize him by the wrist, but Gaynor turned, breaking free of the Sidhi dwarf's grip and aiming at him the blow he had intended for Corum.

For the second time Traitor bit into Goffanon's flesh, and for the second time it remained there as Gaynor, still desperate, began to run, passing at last through the last circle.

Corum crawled to where Goffanon lay. The wound was a bad one. The Sidhi smith's blood rushed from the great gash Traitor had made and was sucked up by the hard earth. Corum tugged the moon-colored blade from Goffanon's side and cradled the great head in his lap. Already the blood was draining from Goffanon's face. The Sidhi was dying. He could not last more than a few moments.

Goffanon said: "The sword was well-named, Vadhagh. It has a fine edge, too."

"Oh, Goffanon . . ." began Corum, but the dwarf shook his head.

"I am glad to die. My time on this plane was over. They have no place for the likes of us, Vadhagh. Not here. Not now. They know it not yet, but the Malibann disease will linger on this plane, long after the Malibann themselves have gone elsewhere. You should leave, if you can . . ."

"I cannot," said Corum. "The woman I love is here."

"As for that . . ." Goffanon began to cough. Then his eyes glazed, then they closed, then his breathing stopped.

Slowly Corum stood up, oblivious of the great wind which still roared about him. He saw that the Fhoi Myore still struggled, but that few of their vassals could be seen.

Amergin came staggering through the wind and gripped Corum's arm. "I saw Goffanon die. If we could get him to Caer Llud when this is done, perhaps the Cauldron will be able to restore his life."

Corum shook his head. "He wished to die," he said.

Amergin accepted this, returning his attention to the inner circle. "The Fhoi Myore resist the vortex, but it has already taken most of their people back to Limbo."

And Corum remembered Jhary and searched for him among the dim shapes and thought he saw him, his arms waving wildly, his face frightened and white, near the altar, but then he was gone.

And then, one by one, the Fhoi Myore vanished and the wind no longer yelled through the monoliths, and the stone circles ceased to whirl round and round, and the Mabden were rising up and they were cheering and rushing forward toward the altar where still sat a small black and white cat and a box of bronze and gold.

Only Corum and Ilbrec held back, standing over the corpse of the Sidhi dwarf.

"He made a prophecy, Ilbrec," said Corum. "He advised us to leave this plane if we could, to go elsewhere. He thought our fates were no longer linked with the Mabden."

"That could be," said Ilbrec. "Now that this is over I think I will return to the peace of the sea, to my father's kingdom. I can celebrate no victories with my old friend Goffanon not here to drink with me and sing the old Sidhi songs with me. Farewell, Corum." He placed a giant hand upon Corum's shoulder. "Or would you come with me?"

"I love Medhbh," said Corum. "That is why I must remain."

Ilbrec got slowly into Splendid Mane's saddle and without further ceremony began to ride over the snow-covered plain, heading back into the West.

Only Corum saw him depart.

The Fifth Chapter

THE RETURN TO CASTLE OWYN

They had come back to Caer Llud to find the winter faded and a kind of spring in its place, and although there were many ruins to rebuild and many corpses to burn with due ceremony upon the stone pyres on the outskirts of the city, and although there remained, here and there, many signs of the Fhoi Myore occupation of the Mabden capital, they were still joyful. And Amergin went to the great tower where he had once been held prisoner under an enchantment (and from where Corum had rescued him) and he found the Cauldron and he found his Collar of Power and he displayed them to all the Mabden who had come with him back to Caer Llud. And he offered them as proof that the Fhoi Myore were gone forever from the land, that Old Night was surely banished.

And they honored Corum as a great hero who had saved their race. And they made up songs concerning his three quests, his deeds and his courage, but Corum found that he could not smile, that he could feel no elation, only sadness, for he mourned for Jhary-a-Conel, banished to Limbo with the Fhoi Myore, and he mourned for the Sidhi dwarf Goffanon, slain by the sword called Traitor.

Soon after they had arrived at Caer Llud, Amergin took the small black and white cat and the box of bronze and gold away with him to the top of his tower, and during the night there was a dry storm, and much lightning and thunder, but no rain, and eventually, in the morning, Amergin emerged from his tower without the box of bronze and gold, but holding the trembling body of the cat, and he told Corum that the bargain with the Malibann had been completed. Corum took the cat, which no longer had Sactric's eyes, and kept it ever with him.

Then, when the first celebrations were over, Corum went to Amergin and bade farewell to the High King, saying that he had it in mind to return to Caer Mahlod with those of the Tuha-na-Cremm Croich still alive, and that the woman he loved, Queen Medhbh, also wished this. So Amergin thanked Corum once more and said that soon he, too, would visit Caer Mahlod, for there were still many things they could fruitfully discuss, and Corum said that he looked forward with pleasure to Amergin's visit. Then they left.

They rode back into the West and they saw that the West was green again, though the animals were slow in returning and the farms were deserted and there were nothing but corpses in the villages, and then they came to Caer Mahlod, the fortress city on the conical hill, close to the oak grove and not far from the sea, and they were there for several days before Medhbh woke one morning and leaned over Corum and stroked his head and said to him:

"You have changed, my love. You are so grim."

"Forgive me," he said. "I love you, Medhbh."

"I forgive you," she told him. "And I love you, Corum." But there was a note of hesitation in her voice and her eyes looked away into a distance. "I love you," she said again. She kissed him.

And a night or two later he lay again in bed and he awoke from a nightmare in which he had seen his own face all twisted with malice and he heard a harp playing somewhere beyond the walls of Caer Mahlod and he looked to wake Medhbh and tell her of it, but she was not in the bed and when he sought her out he could find her nowhere. He asked her, in the morning, where she had been, but she told him that he must have awakened from one dream into another, that she had been at his side all the night.

And the next night he woke up and he saw that she lay sleeping peacefully beside him, but he had a mind to get up (he did not know why) and put on all his armor, and to strap his sword, Traitor, around him. And he went out of the castle, leading the Yellow Stallion, and he mounted the steed and turned its head toward the sea and he rode until he reached the cliff which had broken away, leaving an isolated peak on which stood the ruins of a place called by the Mabden Castle Owyn and by him Castle Erorn, where he had been born and where, until the coming of the old Mabden, he had been happy.

And Corum bent his head to the ear of the Yellow Stallion and said to that noble, ugly horse: "You have great strength, horse of Laegaire, and you have great intelligence. Could you leap this gulf and take me to Castle Erorn?"

And the Yellow Stallion turned his warm, marigold-colored eyes to look at Corum, and there was not amusement there but concern, and the Yellow Stallion snorted and pawed the ground.

"Do this, Yellow Stallion," said Corum, "and I will free you to return to whence you came."

And the Yellow Stallion hesitated, then seemed to agree. He turned and trotted back toward Caer Mahlod, then turned again and began to gallop, faster and faster, until the gulf between the mainland and the promontory on which Castle Owyn stood was very close, and the spray was white in the moonlight and the sea boomed like the voice of a banished Fhoi Myore, and the Yellow Stallion tensed himself, then leapt and his hooves came down squarely upon the rock on the other side and at last Corum had achieved his ambition. He dismounted.

Then the Yellow Stallion looked enquiringly at him and Corum said simply: "You are free, upon the same conditions that Laegaire made." And the Yellow Stallion nodded his head and turned and leapt again across the gulf and was gone into the darkness. And over the sound of the sea Corum thought he heard a voice calling to him from the battlements of Caer Mahlod. Was it Medhbh's voice that called?

He ignored the voice. He stood there and he contemplated the old, worn walls of Castle Erorn, and he remembered how the Mabden had killed his family and then maimed him, taking away his hand and his eye, and he wondered, for a moment, why he had served them so long and so fully. It seemed ironic to him then that, in both cases, it had been largely for the love of Mabden women. But there was a difference between Rhalina and Queen Medhbh that he could not understand, though he loved them both, and they had loved him.

He heard a movement from within the ruined walls and he stepped closer, wondering if he would see again the youth with the face and limbs of gold whom he had seen there once and who was called Dagdagh. He saw a shadow move, glimpsed scarlet in the moonlight, called out:

"Who's there?"

There was no reply.

He stepped closer until his hand touched the time-smoothed carving of the portal, and he hesitated before he went further, saying again:

"Who's there?"

And something hissed like a snake. And something clicked. And something rattled. And Corum saw that the body of a man was outlined against the light which entered through a ruined window, and the man turned and his face was revealed to Corum.

It was Corum's face. It was Calatin's changeling, his Karach, smelling of brine. And the Karach smiled and drew its sword.

"I greet you, brother," said Corum. "I knew in my bones that the prophecy would be fulfilled tonight. I think that that is why I came."

And the Karach said nothing, only smiled, and in the distance now Corum heard the sweet, sinister tones of the Dagdagh harp.

"But what," said Corum, "is the beauty I must fear?"

And he drew his sword, Traitor, out.

"Do you know, changeling?" he asked.

But the changeling's smile merely broadened a little to show white teeth the exact match of Corum's.

"I think I would have my robe back now," said Corum. "I know that I must fight you for it."

And they came together, then, fighting, and their swords struck bright sparks in the gloom of the castle's interior. As Corum had guessed, they were perfectly balanced, skill for skill, strength for strength.

They fought all over the cracked floor of Castle Erorn. They fought over slabs of broken masonry. They fought on half-fallen stairways. They fought for an hour, matching blow for blow, cunning for cunning, but now Corum understood that the changeling had one advantage. He was tireless.

The wearier Corum became the more energetic the changeling seemed to be. He did not speak (perhaps he could not speak) but his smile grew imperceptibly broader and increasingly mocking.

Corum fell back, depending more and more upon defensive swordplay. The changeling drove him out of the door of Castle Erorn, drove him to the very edge of the cliff, until Corum gathered his strength and lunged forward, taking the changeling by surprise and grazing his arm with Traitor.

The changeling did not seem to feel the wound, renewing his attack with vigor.

Then Corum's heel struck a rock and he stumbled backward and he fell, his sword flying from his hand, and he cried out in a miserable voice:

"This is unjust! This is unjust!"

And the harp began to sound again and it seemed to sing a song with words. He thought it sang:

"Ah, the world was ever so. How sad are heroes when their tasks are done . . ."

As if savoring its victory, the changeling moved slowly forward, raising its sword.

Corum felt a tugging at his left wrist. It was his silver hand and it had come alive of its own volition. He saw the straps and the pins loosen, he saw the silver hand rise up and travel swiftly to where Traitor lay, glowing in the moonlight.

"I am mad," said Corum. But he recalled how Medhbh had taken his hand away to put a charm upon it. He had forgotten, as, no doubt, had she.

Now the silver hand, which Corum had fashioned himself, took hold of the Sidhi-forged sword while the changeling looked wide-eyed at it and hissed, stumbling away from it, moaning.

And the silver hand drove the sword Traitor deep into the changeling's heart and the changeling yelled and fell and was dead.

Corum laughed.

"Farewell, brother! I was right to fear you, but you did not bring me my doom!"

The harp sounded louder now, coming from within the castle. Forgetful of his sword and his silver hand, Corum ran back into the castle, and there stood the Dagdagh, a youth all of gold, with sharp, beautiful features and deep, sardonic eyes, and he played upon a harp which seemed in some way to grow out of him and into him and was part of his body. And behind the Dagdagh Corum saw another whom he recognized, and it was Gaynor.

Corum wished that he had not forgotten his sword. He said:

"How I hate you, Gaynor. You slew Goffanon."

"Inadvertently. I have come to make peace with you, Corum."

"Peace? You are my most terrible enemy and ever shall be!"

"Listen to the Dagdagh," said Gaynor the Damned. And the Dagdagh spoke—or rather he sang—and he said this to Corum:

"You are not welcome, mortal. Take your name-robe from the changeling's corpse and leave this world. You were brought here for one purpose. Now that purpose is achieved you must go."

"But I love Medhbh," said Corum. "I will not leave her!"

"You loved Rhalina and you see her in Medhbh."

Gaynor said urgently: "I speak without malice, Corum. Believe the Dagdagh. Come with me now. He has opened a door into a land where we can both know

158

peace. It is true, Corum, I have been there briefly. Here is our chance to see an end to the eternal struggle."

Corum shook his head. "Perhaps you speak the truth, Gaynor. I see truth in the Dagdagh's eyes, too. But I must stay here. I love Medhbh."

"I have spoken to Medhbh," said the Dagdagh. "She knows that it is wrong for you to remain in this world. You do not belong. Come, now, to the land where you and Gaynor will know contentment. It is a great reward I offer you, Eternal Champion. It is more than I could normally achieve."

"I must stay," said Corum.

The Dagdagh began to play upon his harp. The music was sweet and it was euphoric. It was the music of noble love, of selfless heroism. Corum smiled.

He bowed to the Dagdagh, thanking him for what he had offered, and he made a sign of farewell to Gaynor. Then he walked out of the old doorway of Castle Erorn and he saw that Medhbh was waiting for him on the other side. He smiled at her, lifting his right hand in greeting.

But she did not smile back. There was something in her own right hand which she now raised above her head and began to whirl. It was a sling. He looked at her in surprise. Did she seek to slay the Dagdagh, in whom she had put so much trust?

Something left the sling and struck him upon the forehead and he fell down, but he still lived, though his heart was in agony and his head was cracked. He felt the blood pour down his face.

And he saw that the Dagdagh loomed over him, looking down on him with an expression of sympathy. And Corum snarled at the Dagdagh.

"Fear a harp," said the Dagdagh in his high, sweet voice, "fear beauty," and he glanced across the chasm to where Medhbh stood weeping, "and fear a brother . . ."

"Your harp it was that turned Medhbh's heart against me," said Corum. "I was right to fear that. And I should have feared her beauty, for it is what has destroyed me. But I slew the brother, I slew the Karach."

"No," said the Dagdagh, and he picked up the tathlum which Medhbh had hurled. "Here is your brother, Corum. His brain she mixed with lime to make the only thing which fate would allow to slay you. She took the brain from under the mound, from the mound of Cremm Croich, and, on my instructions, she made it. Cremm Croich slays Corum Llaw Ereint. You did not have to die."

"I could not deny her love," Corum managed to rise to his feet and put his left hand to his cracked skull, feeling the blood flow over it. "I love her still."

"I spoke to her. I told her what I would offer you and what she must do if you refused that offer. You have no place here, Corum."

"So say you!" Corum gathered his strength and he lunged at the Dagdagh, but the youth of gold made a sign and Corum's silver hand appeared, still clutching the moon-colored sword Traitor.

And Corum heard Medhbh utter a shriek before the sword entered his heart at exactly the same spot it had entered the changeling's.

And he heard the Dagdagh say:

"Now this world is free of all sorcery and all demigods."

Then Corum died.

THIS ENDS THE THIRD AND FINAL VOLUME
OF THE CHRONICLE OF CORUM
AND THE SILVER HAND